D1493812

...ODAY bestselling and RITA® Award-nominated
Caitlin Crews loves writing romance. She
...her favourite romance novels in creative writing
...at places like UCLA Extension's Prestigious
...Programme, where she finally gets to utilise the
...PhD in English Literature she received from
...versity of York in England. She currently lives
...cific Northwest, with her very own hero and
...pets. Visit her at caitlincrews.com.

KIDNAPPED BY THE VIKING

Caitlin Crews

MILLS & BOON

First Published in Great Britain 2021
by Mills & Boon, an imprint of HarperCollins*Publishers*
1 London Bridge Street, London, SE1 9GF

© 2021 Caitlin Crews

ISBN: 978-0-263-28396-9

For my favorite professor Mark Amodio,
who taught me to love Old English literature long, long ago.

Chapter One

❧❧❧

"…she was deprived of all authority and
taken into Wessex."

—*The Life of Aelfwynn,*
Daughter of the only Lady of the Mercians
as recorded in the *Anglo-Saxon Chronicle,*
918 AD

The Northman stood in the middle of the old
road like a mountain of stone and dread, a
giant blocking the way through the darkening wood.

At first Aelfwynn thought she was hallu-
cinating him. It had been so many hours of
cold, uncomfortable riding from the fortified
burh of Tamworth where she had watched her
mother, the much-beloved Lady of the Mercians, die six months ago. They had set off before first light, setting a brisk pace despite the

season's wintry fog. Aelfwynn had felt every muddy, frozen, treacherous bump too well this sad day, due in part to the tired old horse that was all her uncle had allotted her for the long, hard journey south into his grand kingdom of Wessex. But her heart was heavy, and that made every ache and pain seem the greater.

Her mind had danced away from what awaited her in the new, quiet life she would start at Wilton Abbey. Her heart had longed for what she left behind, what she'd lost, what could never be regained.

And then he had appeared like a nightmare.

A nightmare Aelfwynn had suffered through many times, both waking and sleeping, thanks to the many battles she had witnessed in her lifetime—or had not witnessed personally— yet was forced to wait in dire apprehension to see who would return and who would not. She was a grandchild of the great King Alfred of Wessex. She had been born of his eldest daughter Aethelflaed and was her royal mother's only issue. Fighting off the many savages who rose against them in repeated attempts to take their lands and call themselves its rulers had consumed them all for as long as anyone could recall.

She blamed the relentless scourge of Northmen like this one—or the terrible Danes, or the bloody Norse—for the loss of her mother this past June and her elderly father seven years before. These hostile, warfaring men from the east, their havoc and their raids and their conquests, never truly stopped. *Conquer them in the west and they rise again in the east,* her mother had always said. *Then north, then south.* The only constant was bloodshed.

Always and ever the bloodshed, staining the very earth beneath Aelfwynn's feet.

But blame and blood alike did naught to clear her path this evening.

This Northman was broad and tall, dressed in furs and wool that did nothing to conceal the truth of him. That he was a warrior was obvious in the way he held himself, a silent yet distinct threat. The snow that had been falling bleakly since the frigid midday settled on his wide shoulders, dusting his head and dark beard, but he appeared to notice neither that nor the rearing mounts of the two men of questionable strength her uncle had grudgingly spared for her.

Instead his gaze, a dark and powerful force, hit Aelfwynn like a blow, making her glad she had the hood of her own cloak to hide her in some small way. Though she knew that no bandit would mistake her for a commoner, even without the men guarding her on this journey. She rode a horse instead of walking, for one. And her clothes were too fine. Her cloak and the headdress beneath, wrapped around her head and neck, were wool—and she only hoped he could not see the finely wrought jeweled pins that held her headdress in place that would as good as shout out who she was to the whole of the kingdom.

"Stand down!" cried one of her uncle's men.

A bit late, to Aelfwynn's mind.

The Northman did not yield. He gave as much notice to the order as did the stark trees that lined the road.

"We travel under the banner of King Edward of Wessex," cried the other. "Dare you court his displeasure?"

"And yet I see no king before me," said the Northman, his voice a low, rough rumble that made Aelfwynn feel almost dizzy, so much so that her skittish old horse began to drift sideways, toward the forest where nothing good lurked.

Nothing good left anywhere, it seems, she thought with a touch of self-pity that shamed her even as it swelled in her, *with a giant in the road.* She corrected her mount and strove to cast off her own dark, unworthy thoughts, feeling the warrior's gaze on her all the while.

Aelfwynn wanted nothing more than to shout him down, the way her men had tried— if in voices that betrayed the distinct lack of courage that had likely led her uncle to pick them for this distasteful task of very little glory. She wanted to follow up her orders with the dagger she carried, tucked beneath her clothes as she knew the Northman's own weapons surely were too. But if she'd learned anything in the course of this long, grim year, it was how to hide. If she'd given in to her darker impulses, even once and no matter how good it might have felt, she would not have survived.

She had been raised in her father's court, then served as her mother's foremost companion during the seven years Aethelflaed had ruled after his death. A year ago she had been confident in her place. Her mother had feared nothing, no man and no army. Aethelflaed had taken on the Five Boroughs then held as part of the Danelaw, the agreed-upon territory of the invaders who had ferociously set siege to these lands for more than a hundred years. In the last year the Lady of Mercia had sacked Danish-held Derby, accepted the surrender of Leicester, and had been offered the loyalty of the Christian leaders of York—but had died before she could accept.

Leaving Aelfwynn to carry on in her stead.

But Aelfwynn had long since accepted that she was not her mother. She feared too much—and wore that fear too plainly. Men and armies alike, Danes and Northmen and Saxons and all who had swarmed around her, whispering in her ear about what Mercia must do to distinguish itself from its ally to the south—the Kingdom of Wessex, ruled by her uncle Edward, who considered himself less an ally and more the rightful king who had graciously permitted his sister to wield power at his pleasure.

A favor he did not intend to extend to his niece, particularly when her loyalty could not be as easily assured as that of his sister.

I could marry you to an ally, he had told her when he'd come to claim Tamworth, laying waste to what remained of Mercian dreams of independence and embodying all of Aelfwynn's fears. *But allies have a terrible habit of turning into foes, do they not?*

Had Aelfwynn listened to those who whispered to her, had she acted on what they'd implored her to do or even spoken forthrightly in his presence as her mother would have done without a second thought, he would have treated her like one of those foes. No one would have blamed him.

Well did she know this. Her silence—the meekness she wrapped around her like a thick, woolen cloak no matter how she felt within or how the heaviness of it scratched at her skin—had saved her. It was why she was even now headed to live out her days at an abbey when her uncle could far more easily have killed her.

No one would have blamed him for that, either.

This is mercy, niece, he had told her when he had rendered his decision, his gaze a glittering thing, not quite malice and yet nothing near affection, either. *My gift to you, in memory of my sister.*

Then, as now, Aelfwynn bowed her head when some small part of her longed to follow her fearless mother's example and fight. Lead armies. Raze cities. Control kingdoms. Strike down her enemies and make them cower before her—but there had been only one Lady of the Mercians. Aelfwynn was all too aware she could only ever be a disappointment in comparison. She had been.

And not only because what she truly wanted was not these games of war, but peace.

Thus she did now, as she always had, using what few tools she had at her disposal. She made herself small and seemingly pious, her prayers a pretty melody in her best church Latin against the falling night.

"I have come for your lady," the Northman told her uncle's men, his voice neither pretty nor melodic and yet the effect was much the same. He still didn't move, as if he truly was hewn from stone. "I have no quarrel with you. Yet rise against me or attempt to stop me here and I will paint the trees with your blood."

His voice was so quiet and dark, his prayer a threat, that it made Aelfwynn's very skin pull tight. A chill ran through her. Yet all she could do was what she had done since her mother died. Keep her head down and hope that once again, the forces she couldn't possibly fight took pity on her instead. Whatever it took to stay alive.

The Northman sized up the men who flanked her, as if their weak characters were stamped up their faces. "If you leave now, no one will ever be the wiser."

"The lady is for Wilton," said one of the guards. Though it came out more a question than a statement. "She is bound for the nunnery by order of the king."

"These roads are treacherous in winter," the warrior said quietly. But when Aelfwynn snuck a look at him, his gaze was intense. And trained on her once more. "Bandits and wolves abound, and precious few kings among them. Who can say what tragedies might befall such a delicate creature out here in the dark?"

Aelfwynn's breath shortened. She stopped pretending to pray, because her uncle's men were looking at each other, then back at the Northman, their dread and reluctance all too obvious.

They did not look at her. As if she was incidental to their decision.

"My uncle is a powerful man and Mercia is now his," she reminded them, hoping the formidable giant before them would take heed as well. "Do you dare cross him?"

The warrior regarded her steadily as if the night did not thicken around them. As if he had yet to notice the snow.

As if he already knew how this would end.

"Better to ask yourself if you dare to cross me," he said in a deep, foreboding rumble.

Aelfwynn found she was holding her breath, a strange tumult within her. She did not know if he spoke to her uncle's fearful men—or, more worryingly, to her.

She prayed truly and silently then, that others might come along this way and put a stop to this as her uncle's men could not. Though she knew too well only fools and monsters would be out in this weather, so far from shelter on a night like this. And it was all too apparent there were both on this lonely stretch of ancient road, herself the greatest fool of all for imagining she might escape the grief and chaos of this darkest year unscathed.

In truth, she should not have been surprised when the two men—still without so much as a glance in her direction—turned their mounts around in a flurry of kicks and cries, then galloped back the way they'd come. Cowards to the end.

Aelfwynn hastily cast off her shroud of meekness, kicking her poor old nag—

But he was there, the great giant of a Northman, without seeming to move at all. He took the reins from her—and control of her useless mount—that easily. And then he waited, gazing at her with that same darkly fierce calm, very much as if he was daring her to fight him when her men had not.

She had a knife strapped at her thigh, the bands digging into the hose she wore on her legs. But how could she reach it with him *right there?* She doubted he would stand idly by as she dug beneath her outer woolen cloak and the under cloak beneath it, trimmed in fur. Much less her pretty dress with its embroidery and the necklaces that had been her mother's, or the linen underdress against her skin—all before she could access her knife while seated high on her horse.

He was too big, too close. He would stop her as he'd stopped her useless horse, and there was a gleam in his dark gaze that made her wonder if he knew not only that she carried a knife, but precisely where she had secreted it

on her person before she'd left Tamworth this
morn. It only made her that much more aware
of how powerful and dangerous he was, even
without the weapons she could now glimpse
beneath his cloak.

"Release me now," she said with as much
dignity as she could manage when her hands
shook. "And I promise, no harm will come
to you."

He considered her. "But what are your
promises worth when you cannot defend
them? Nor yourself?"

Aelfwynn folded her hand into the folds of
her thick outer cloak so the Northman could
not see her shake. She longed to draw the
drapery of her headdress over her face but
dared not. She knew too well how fear en-
flamed men's darker passions and knew better
than to fan those flames herself. She thought
of her mother, battle-ready and ever cool, and
inclined her head.

It made her belly twist a bit, deep inside,
that he was so much bigger and taller than
most men and she did not need to look too
far down to meet his gaze.

"It is as my men told you. My uncle is
Edward, King of Wessex." She waited for

some expression of awe or fear, in case he had missed both the banner her men had carried with its golden dragon and her uncle's name. No awe or fear appeared on the warrior's countenance, like carved stone. "He is of late in Tamworth, almost a full day's ride from here, and he will not look favorably upon it should I come to harm."

"Is that so?" He sounded almost amused, though there was little hint of it on his harsh face. His attention never wavered. "Your uncle does not look upon you with favor, Lady Aelfwynn. Or he would not have stripped you of your birthright and taken Mercia for his own, would he?"

She went cold, then hot. Terror made her lips numb, no matter how she tried to tell herself it was the snow. "How is it you know me?"

"Who does not know you?" the Northman asked with a certain quiet menace, a gleam in his dark eyes that she could not read. But she could feel it as if he'd set his hands upon her flesh. "You possess a greater claim to Mercia than the man who calls it his, yet live."

She knew she did not imagine the hard emphasis he put on those last two words.

Aelfwynn held herself still, trying not to panic. She wished she dared fling herself from the back of the horse he held placid and docile, as if both it and she were his. If she risked the jump and the landing, she could run off and take her chances in the looming woods. But the Northman had not been wrong about this lonely place. These roads were dangerous even in the bright light of a summer's day. But tonight it was three weeks before midwinter. She would find nothing in these stark, watchful trees save a choice of brutal deaths.

In the distance, a wolf howled, and Aelfwynn could not contain the shudder that moved through her at the desolate sound.

"You would do well to question what your uncle had planned for you," the warrior told her. He indicated the woods, the road. The last of the pale light that hovered low in the trees, a grim warning. "The night comes, yet you are nowhere near shelter. If you had been set upon, what defense could your men have offered? I ran them off without so much as drawing a weapon."

I have been set upon, she thought while her heart pounded. *By a Northman.*

What manner of man was this, to offer

her calm words and strange riddles when he could so easily cut her down instead? When she could see the dark havoc in his gaze and knew him for what he was—a man as unlike the two who had abandoned her here as it was possible to be. A man who could take on the woods, the wolves, and any other threat he pleased.

A savage Northman who would not hesitate to spill blood, claim spoils, and pillage as he wished.

"What good is it to tell every truth," Aelfwynn managed to murmur, wishing the old words her mother had always said brought a better comfort this night. But the cold and her panic and his pitiless gaze were taking hold no matter how she tried to fight it.

"A fine saying." The Northman's hard mouth curved and she felt it scald her insides, a fire and a shout at once. "Will it save you, do you think?"

Aelfwynn searched his face, his punishing and steady gaze, for a mercy that wasn't there. This close, she could not help but notice details about him that seemed to lodge themselves beneath her skin. That his hair was dark beneath the snow, fixed in braids that kept it from his face. His beard was the same rich shade, threaded through with more snow that he appeared to notice not at all. His gaze was dark too, and stirring, though his eyes had the look of midnight—a deep, rich blue. He was a harsh warrior, this much was evident, but he was regrettably not as hideously brutish as Aelfwynn might have liked.

On the contrary, he was hard to look away from. He had moved so swiftly, despite his size. And he held himself in the way some men did, as if they were a thing that happened to the earth and not the opposite.

He was as magnificent as he was terrifying, and Aelfwynn was entirely within his power.

Her mother had been raised on military tactics handed down by her own father, King Alfred, who had routed the scourge of Northmen, Norse, and Danes aplenty in his day. Aethelflaed had always expected she would one day command armies and had prepared for it, in study and action, including her infamous decree that having borne her husband a single child a near decade into their union, she would risk herself in childbirth no more.

She would have advised her daughter to plot, not panic.

Aelfwynn missed her grievously.

But her uneasy months of politics and pretense were behind her now. There was only this man and the woods, the song of the wolves, and a reckoning here in the coming cold night whether she wanted it or did not. She could not pray it away. She could not outrun it.

He had captured her without unsheathing his sword. That was her shame to bear.

And bear it she would, if only she lived, out in the dark with a knife she couldn't reach to wield on a horse that would not run, her uncle's men long gone, and safety a mere story told around fires in the halls of her youth. She had left all she knew behind and what remained was…herself.

Only and ever herself.

Something shifted in her, then. A plot, perhaps. Not that blind panic that made her feel as frozen as the old road below her.

I am my mother's daughter, Aelfwynn told herself. *Whether I look it or not.*

And to prove it, she did not shrink from the man who watched her so closely, his gaze too knowing, too bold.

Instead, she smiled.

"I doubt you are lingering in a darkened wood, covered in snow while the weather worsens, to play the savior. You will save me or kill me as it pleases you, I dare say, and well do both of us and the wolves themselves know it."

She sounded cool and disinterested when inside, Aelfwynn felt lit on fire. But she did not let her smile drop, for hers was the blood of kings and queens of old, and she too would fight.

In the only way she could.

The Northman's midnight eyes blazed.

Aelfwynn did not look away. "Yet you need only tell me what I must do to stay your hand, and I will do it."

Chapter Two

Eigi fellr tré við it fyrsta högg.

A tree does not fall with the first blow.

—*Njáls Saga,* common usage

She was not what he'd expected.

Thorbrand had spent the last half of this long year working toward this day. He, his brother Ulfric and their cousin Leif had been tasked with this undertaking by none other than the mighty Ragnall, their king long hated and feared by these Mercians. The three of them had been little more than untried youths when the Irish kings had expelled their people from Dublin. They had grown into fierce and loyal men together, forged in the wicked fire of one battle after another throughout these long and bloody seasons. They were kin, good friends, and battle-honed brothers. Feared and fearsome warriors in their own right, they had fought for glory, honor, and territory at Ragnall's side from the Isle of Man into Northumbria, back to Ireland to reclaim what had been taken some fifteen years ago, then back to this bitter island and straight into border skirmishes with the vicious Scots earlier this year.

That last battle at Corbridge had whetted Ragnall's appetite for deception, as he'd led the column that had laid in wait until the Scots thought they'd defeated the rest, only to surge forth and claim their victory. Ragnall had started thinking less of what he could smash with his fists or cut down with his axe, and more of the other games he could play to achieve his ends.

And which among his loyal men could be best trusted to bring his cleverest schemes to life.

It was nothing less than an honor, Thorbrand had reminded himself throughout this long season of planning and plotting, to serve his king in this plot made of waiting. Not in the sharp fire of a straightforward battle, all sword heft and might, but in this deeper plot that would test Thorbrand's skills in new ways.

Yet the gods knew well that in his heart, he had not felt honored by this assignment.

Then again, he had expected the Lady Aelfwynn to cower and mewl as these Saxon noblewomen did, sending up their frantic prayers to their Christian god and fainting into the mud when their prayers went unanswered.

Better to have a selection of gods, Thorbrand had always thought. Lest one alone prove uninterested in providing aid, as the fickle gods so often did.

Aelfwynn had prayed with her old Roman words, but he had seen no cowering. Instead, she looked at him directly. The challenge of it stirred his blood. Thorbrand was a warrior, not a weakling, and he hungered for the bold, strong warrior women his people bred. Not these grim, cold Christians with their bloodless piety.

And yet this woman, this Mercian princess he was tasked to take no matter what he thought of her, begged a second look.

She almost reminded him—

But he cast such thoughts aside. His past could have no purpose here. What was done could not be altered with memories. Well did Thorbrand know this.

"Do you offer yourself to me?" His question was little more than a dark scrape of sound. He kept his gaze trained on her lovely face beneath the headwrap and hood she wore against the cold night, searching for the fear he'd expected to see there. But did not.

Not that she wasn't fearful, alone in the dark here with a man she would likely think a monster. He was close enough now that he could see the way she trembled slightly, though her eyes—eyes that gleamed gold, and what man was not partial to whatever gold he could hoard?—did not leave his.

She is brave, Thorbrand thought then, pleased.

And it was far too tempting to imagine what an offering might look like. How it might feel to find his ease deep between her thighs.

"Can a woman offer what has already been claimed by the threat of force in the middle of a dark wood?" Aelfwynn asked, a trace of wry humor in her voice.

Surprising Thorbrand anew. And with that surprise came a new surge of heat. "A woman can always offer. Who does not like a gift freely given?"

"I will confess a certain wariness when

it comes to gifts," she replied, her gaze still steady. She sat straight and tall before him, nothing like the woman he'd seen at first. The one who had bowed her head, then meekly murmured her prayers. Thorbrand found himself more intrigued by the moment and his blood answered that fascination by coursing through him like a newly kindled fire. "I find that the greater the gift, the more obligation expected in return. Is that not so?"

She reminded him of similar words he'd heard spoken in the longhouses of his childhood. It was unsettling. He had not expected she would be anything like him, this almost-queen who was more valuable for what she represented than anything else. She had been stripped of her lands, her people. She had been shunted off from her uncle's court and could easily have faded off into obscurity in a nunnery, a tale seldom told. Absent from songs and stories evermore, no threat to anyone. He had not expected her to be anything but female goods he would carry off to faraway shores and find a way to live with, eventually. In some or other peace, gods willing—but live with her he would, peace or no.

Not that Thorbrand knew much of peace.

Or would recognize it if it fell upon him like a battle-ax.

"The way of the world is unlikely to be changed here in this wood," he said gruffly.

But he was speaking to himself as much as to her. He could not forget himself here, even if she compelled him more than he'd ever imagined she would. Even if she somehow prodded at memories he had done his best to banish. He knew what business he had with this woman—and would have had even if she'd toppled from her horse in a fright and had cringed about before him in the frozen dirt at his feet.

His orders had to do with his king's desires, not his own. Never his own.

He should not have tarried while carrying out this errand, yet Thorbrand did not move. He stayed where he was, gazing at her as she sat before him. Almost proudly, he thought, like the queen she might have been. And nearly had been, these last six months, to her uncle's fury. "Tell me, Aelfwynn, what will you offer me for your life?"

"Is it I who determines what my life is worth?" She inclined her head but slightly. "Or is it he who would take it?"

Thorbrand knew these games. And misliked them. Words like swords, the lifeblood of a royal court, where whispers could poison and rumors could kill. It was good to remember that she had these weapons, little as he might value them. Not when he could measure the world by the swing of his sword.

And did.

"Such philosophical words, lady." He saw her jaw firm even as she trembled and told himself it was good. Better she should fear him than imagine she could tie him in knots with pretty words. "And yet the snow still falls. The wolves yet howl. And where, do you think, might you lay your head this night?"

Aelfwynn laughed and it startled him, when he was a man so hardened he would have sworn to the gods themselves that there was naught on this dark, doomed earth that could catch him unawares. It was her laughter. That she dared laugh in the first place, and more, the sound of it. It put him in mind of a crisp, cold stream, tumbling from the mountains in the new land called Ísland—that place far to the west he had first seen this summer and now carried in him, as if those mountains like slumbering dragons and black rock beaches had claimed him that quickly.

When he intended to do the claiming.

Because sooner or later, all men needed land.

Trouble was, all the land Thorbrand had ever known was soaked in blood. Battled over, taken again and again, no sword mighty enough to beat back those who would challenge a man's right to settle. No war ever truly over, no truce anything but uneasy though even a hundred years might pass. Or more.

Thorbrand had never had a home he was not called upon to defend with his body, his sword, the strength in his arms and the will in his heart.

And too well did he know the things a man could lose when his strength was outmatched, his sword overpowered, his will not enough. Well did he remember that bloody morning in Dublin when he had failed.

Gods, how he had failed.

Too vividly did he recall the look on his mother's face when she had fallen that day. When he had not protected her as he should have done. When the enemy had tossed him aside like a child when he had been a man of fifteen, then cut her down while he had watched and had done nothing.

The shame of that haunted him still.

His mother had been brave and bold, beautiful and clever. She had given his father sons and had feared little. When other women might have begged to be spared, his mother had gone at her attacker as if she'd intended to take his eyes out.

She had fought for her home, but it had been burned down all the same.

Thorbrand had never told anyone what he had witnessed. What he had failed to do that bitter day when the Irish kings had routed his people from the only home many of them had ever known, ordering them to leave Ireland. Or die.

He had told himself he did not look for a home, not when his had been taken from him and turned to ash along with the mother he had not saved. He had told himself that all his years since had been his atonement. For in the wake of that day, Thorbrand had learned to fight—far harder and much better than he had as a boy.

To fight. To win. To put himself on the line again and again.

To do what he had failed to do then, when it had counted the most.

He had long believed that this was what he must do, as penance and proof to the gods. To make up for what he had not done then.

And yet, in these ever-desperate times, he sometimes found himself wondering if there was something more to life than the grim, ceaseless march of so many bloody skirmishes. The cry of battle, the clash of steel. He sometimes dreamed of a home. A true home, not a tent tossed up in another encampment, too near to yet another battleground. A place where he could live instead of fight, battle-weary but free.

Though thinking thus, he knew, was his own great and bitter shame. A man fought until the gods took him, dreaming of Valhalla all the while. A man longed for the honor only found in the fight. And on that dark day, long ago, Thorbrand had pledged that he would never stop fighting as he wished he could have then. Never.

He was not a soft man who dreamed of farms and seasons, the yield of the land and the call of his livestock. Thorbrand had risen from the ashes that day and become a weapon.

It shamed him that he wanted anything more in this bleak life than that.

And still this Saxon lady laughed, as if she had no fear at all. As if she found her own peril amusing.

Very much as his own mother had that hateful day.

"I am pleased I amuse you," he said to Lady Aelfwynn when her laughter stopped, and he did not heed the strange tightening in his chest at the loss of it. He would add it to the rest of his collection, his shame and reproach. His own personal *knarr*, not piled high with goods as the merchant ships usually were, but instead laden with his regrets. "That will make our dealings the easier."

Her golden gaze clung to his. "Then you do not intend to kill me. Is it ransom you are after?"

"Ransom?" He did not laugh, but when his mouth curved her breath came fast enough that he could see the clouds of it upon the air. "I fear you overestimate your worth to your uncle. Had he wished to protect you, would he have sent you on your way in this fashion? Two cowards as some faint enough protection, fat pouches begging for a bandit's attention, and nothing but your prayers to protect you?"

Though color bloomed in her cheeks, Aelfwynn did not wilt at that, either. "It is not mine to question the decisions my uncle has made. As he is also my king."

"Then I will question him for you, and gladly. He is not *my* king."

She did not so much as flinch when Thorbrand had expected tears. Cowering. And not because she was a woman, for he had been raised on stories of shield maidens and Valkyries. His own mother had taught him courage, then proved hers beyond any doubt. But the tales of the Lady of Mercia's disappointing daughter had spread wide since June. The Mercian Queen—and it was no matter that technically, she had been no queen but merely the royal wife of an ealdorman, not when she had commanded armies as any true queen might—had been a worthy foe. The daughter, it was said with no little scorn, had done naught but bow her head and retreat into prayer when it was a ruler needed.

All would have been different had she been a son. For one thing, Thorbrand would not have been sent on this errand. He would have been sent to fight, and not like this.

But there were different ways to win wars, as well he knew.

"Am I not to learn my fate, then?" she asked boldly, as if she knew the direction of his thoughts.

"We all learn our fate when it is delivered unto us," he replied. "And none of your prayers will alter what is to come, lady. It is already decided."

"Yet somehow I feel certain the decision about my fate lies in your hands," she replied with that maddening, compelling coolness.

"I will not ransom you to your uncle," Thorbrand told her. He studied her there, the snow turning her dark, rich cloak white. "Surely you must realize he sent you to your death."

"I fear I am but a simple woman caught up in the affairs of kings," she replied after a moment, though the steady way she continued to hold his gaze told him what she said was a lie. She might be any number of things, this Saxon princess, but simple was not among them. "It was my mother who dabbled in the politics of all these warring men. I prefer more gentle arts. I find there is less blood in spinning or needlework."

He shifted where he stood, his hand on the horse's neck. He could have moved closer if he chose. He could have put his hand on her and taught her the folly of lying to him. Something in him roared out in a sudden surge of pure need—but he only stood as he was.

Because a wise man did not use a hammer when a feather would do.

"The world is shaped by blood," he told her bluntly. Much of it his own, the blood he had drawn in turn, and the blood that stained his own hands whether he had drawn it or not. "And your blood marks you a prize to any who might seek it. For as long as you live, there must surely remain doubt that Edward controls Mercia."

She finally flinched, though quickly did she move to conceal it. And Thorbrand found it did not please him as he'd imagined it would.

You do not want this woman scared, a voice inside him intoned, as if from the gods above. *You want her beneath you, joy-filled and bright.*

"There is no doubt," she replied, wariness moving over her face and creeping into the way she held herself stiffer, then. Braced against his words. "I am to take holy vows, prostrating myself before God alone. Leaving these kingdoms to the whims of those who would rule them."

Did he see the hint of a wistfulness about her then? As if she had wanted such a life? Thorbrand did not see the appeal. What use was there in a life dedicated to a god if it must be spent in unnatural silence, hidden away from the world? That did not strike Thorbrand as any kind of life at all.

But it mattered little in her case, for she was not meant for such vows, holy or not. "You would never have reached your abbey, Aelfwynn. I tell you this as a friend."

Something flared on her face then. A flash of temper, he thought, and liked it far better than fear. Or wistfulness for a nunnery. He had always longed for fire and ice, storms and high seas. High temper made his blood sing— it was softness he could not abide.

It reminded him of what he'd lost. What he should have saved.

Of the mother who had been willing enough to fight but had also been the only softness he had ever known.

Thorbrand did not care to recall her softness. Better by far to remember her fierceness, flying at the Irish warrior who had come for her as if she were a shield maiden. It was easier to think of her thus.

Though the shame he bore for having lost her, soft or fierce, never eased.

He made as if to scowl at his quarry as if it was her fault when he knew full well it was his. Then reminded himself that he had, a mere moment ago, claimed friendship.

Remember what game it is you play here, he cautioned himself. *And better still, whose game it is.*

Somehow he kept the scowl from his face.

"A friend? Indeed?" Aelfwynn's chin lifted slightly. "Yet you are the one who has stopped my passage."

"I am not the worst thing on this road, I promise you."

"And me with weak men to protect me. Wolves drawing ever nearer and the night closer still. Warriors barring the way. So you have said."

There was that bright color in her cheeks and a deeper gold in her gaze, making him wonder what other ways he could draw out this passion in her. He had not dreamed that such things would factor in this mission. Or at all. He had long ago forgone passion for duty and had called it the better bargain. But. *But.*

Aelfwynn pressed her lips together as if she wanted to say far more. Or as if she knew where his mind—and his flesh—had gone, when surely she could not. "There are no safe roads in any kingdom, I fear. These are treacherous times."

"But in this case the treachery runs deeper than petty traveling complaints." It was becoming more and more difficult not to touch her, but better not to bait a trap by tripping it himself. "Did you not think to wonder why your men did not stop at the last village?"

He saw something in her face that suggested she had indeed wondered thus. "We meant to move swiftly. There is much ground to cover and the winter grows colder by the day."

Thorbrand took that as a reminder that what he did here was not…this. That she was more alluring than he had predicted was a boon, surely. Nothing more. And there was no reason to stand here in the snow while he wrestled with wanting her.

The woman herself. Not what she represented.

Not when he knew he had naught but time ahead to make the wanting sweeter.

No matter who she made him remember.

"Men lie in wait less than an hour's brisk ride ahead," Thorbrand told her then, no longer pretending he was anything but what he was. A warrior so feared that his enemies quaked when they looked upon him. "Had I not stopped you here, you would have been set upon by now. You would not have survived the encounter. The only question is how they would have killed you. And how long they would have taken with you before they left you for dead."

He meant that last part to shock and scare her. But she surprised him again, this delicate princess who he knew had been raised softly in one royal court after the next. Her uncle's, her father's, her mother's. Her own. She had been given servants and a life of ease while all around her battles raged and men died for lands she could have claimed by virtue of her blood alone.

But Aelfwynn did not falter. "There are a great many ways to die. As we will all of us learn, sooner or later."

"I admire that you can face your uncle's treachery with so little fear."

"Is it my uncle's treachery I face? So you tell me, here in a lonely wood. But I have not seen these men." Her gaze lit then, nearly too gold to bear. "For all I know, they could be yours to command. Northmen like you."

Thorbrand found himself grinning that she should use that word like a weapon when it was only one of the names his people had been called for more than a hundred years, or so the *skalds* sang. Not the Danes. No longer quite Norse. Dubgaill sometimes, Finngaill at other times, depending on who was doing the telling—and thus the naming.

They were called monsters almost always.

And more often than not, to his great pleasure, kings.

So long as she called him her master, as he knew full well she would—and soon—she could call him anything she liked.

He lifted his hand, letting loose the reins of the old nag she rode. He saw her eyes widen, her hands shooting forward—

Then she stopped, as if she expected he might cut them off.

"What is this trick?" she asked. "Do you set me free?"

"If you wish," he said.

The wind gusted around them, blowing the snow sideways, and he thought he saw her blink back the sheen of emotion that made her gold-bright eyes gleam.

He kept speaking as her gloved hands crept closer to the reins. "Ahead of you, ten men lie in wait. They left Tamworth a day before you. Call them Northmen, if it pleases you. If calling them so makes you easier with what they plan for you." He nodded in the direction from which she'd come. "Behind you, two men who have proven themselves the rankest of cowards must make certain your uncle thinks they have completed their mission. Do you think they will welcome your approach, should you retreat? And all this, of course, if either they or you live long enough for this undesirable reunion to take place at all. For the wolves are hungry this winter. It makes them bold."

Her brow furrowed. His grin deepened. "Do you think a woman alone stands a chance against any of these foes, Lady Aelfwynn? If so, ride on. But let me remind you that your mother commanded armies. She did not raise a sword and fight in them."

Thorbrand waited, keeping his face hard. Stern. It would have been easier if she'd been a weak, sodden thing. She would have wept, he would have told her what to do, and she would have done it, wailing all the way. He would have regarded her as an object of pity, though none would have been forthcoming.

He found he was not prepared for this Aelfwynn.

Her surrender had never been in doubt, but even so he craved a true capitulation. He wanted her to choose him, here and now.

And then over and over again.

"I have no reason to trust a word you have said," she said after a moment.

But she didn't attempt to gallop off in one direction or another.

"Can you trust anyone?" He did not shift his gaze, nor his stance. "And even if you could, there are only the two of us here. Will you take your chances with me? Or do you imagine you can fight off men and wolves alike with your prayers?"

And he watched, not without pity, as she pulled in a sharp breath. She looked from side to side, as if the woods themselves could help her. Or as if she had only then noticed how very little light remained, sunk low and indifferent in the sullen winter sky.

He knew well the contours of this kind of waiting. Braced for action. Ready to fight. Yet forced to remain still until the signal came.

But knowing it well failed to make the waiting any the easier.

"I am honored that you have offered me safe passage, sir," Aelfwynn said when he'd begun to wonder if she would speak again. She swallowed, her gaze still on the trees all around them. Then she looked at him full on, because she truly was a brave little thing, and well did it please him. "I accept."

Thorbrand felt something swell in him then. A roar of triumph, as if he'd slain a field of enemies—when all he'd done was convince this woman to make a simple choice.

A choice he could have taken from her, and easily, but it was far sweeter to claim her surrender.

Her first surrender, Thorbrand thought with pleasure.

For there would be many more before he was done.

And he would have her beneath him, this he knew.

He moved then, with a show of lethal swiftness that made her gasp.

It was like music to him.

Well did he like it that she might sense the difference between him and those weaklings her uncle had sent to guide her to her death.

He swung up behind her on the old horse, then gathered her against him. It pleased him how she fit with her back pressed to his front, his thighs caging hers, and her bottom pressed snugly into the part of him that ached for her. Her cloak and scarf had slipped and she reached up to pull them back into place, but not before he glimpsed her hair, thick and fair.

Soon, he promised himself, he would wrap that golden hair around his wrist and teach her what she could do on her knees.

These Christians did love their kneeling.

Thorbrand would have her beg for the pleasure they could take in each other. He would have her prayers, those old church words to her jealous god, yet he alone would grant them.

A longing fiercer than any he had ever known roared in him then.

He controlled the confused horse beneath them with one hand, using his other arm to hold Aelfwynn where he wanted her. He could feel her shake, though she held herself with the same proud strength that had impressed him when his feet were on the ground. He could feel her chest move as if she was fighting off fear or emotion—but no sob escaped her lips.

No wailing. No bargaining. No begging.

He liked the way her body felt, flush against his. He liked that he could feel the outline of a blade strapped to one of her thighs, suggesting there was yet more to the Mercian's pious, weakling princess than he'd been led to believe. That could only bode well for what lay ahead of them.

She had not used weapons, yet she had battled with him, fearlessly. Better still, she faced her fear and did not succumb to it. This was good.

If he could ignore the hint of softness that made him wish he could change the past—when too well did he know he could not—all would be well.

He would take her far away to that cold island, those lands of snow and silence. And this was what they would have, these sword-bright exchanges. This was what would light their winters as he waited for Ragnall to call for her—to bring her back to claim her kingdom when Wessex fell.

To use her as a weapon in this endless war.

But first there would be this.

Thorbrand kicked the horse's side, left the road with the captive he was bound to make his own, and took them deep into the waiting wood.

Chapter Three

Ðeah þe earm friond lytel sylle, nim hit to miccles þances.

Though a poor friend may give you little, take it with great thanks.

—from the *Disticha Catonis*,
translated by Eleanor Parker

The woods swallowed them whole.

Aelfwynn was held tight against the Northman, his mighty arm like a band of stone, holding her fast. There was no give in the powerful body behind her. His chest was a stone fortress. His thighs as hard as rocks.

She trembled and knew that it was fear, even as a part of her melted, too.

For she knew too well what fate must await her.

What she could not understand was why this man had spoken with her as he did, playing games with his words and toying with her, when he could have taken what he wanted at any time. Then left her to die there, violated and alone.

That he hadn't made the part of her that felt like an open flame dance all the higher.

"Yield," came his voice from behind her, that low rumble she could not only hear, but feel deep inside her person. As if he was not only surrounding her, but within her. "Or you will hurt yourself."

Aelfwynn could scarcely imagine what he meant. Or why his words seemed to linger inside her.

"Will you sit thus the whole of the ride?" he asked, sounding amused. "Rigid as one of these barren trees?"

It took her a moment or two to comprehend his meaning. She was sitting as straight as she could, doing her best to avoid the unavoidable as he surrounded her. And still she felt…too much of him.

But his amusement pricked at her and she made herself settle back against him. However slightly.

And her reward, or curse, was the low thread of his laughter that moved like heat through her, making her feel connected from the inside out to this man who held her captive and bore her off through the darkening woods—to what end, she knew not.

Surely it would have been far easier to do as he would with her where he'd found her.

She could not understand this Northman at all.

Her mind raced as the night grew darker, the snow heavier. It was a sad truth that Aelfwynn knew more than she wished to know of men. What woman could avoid such knowledge? Men roamed the earth as they pleased, sacking cities and claiming them in turn, issuing royal coin and commands as they went. And when they were finished cutting down their enemies and demanding songs sung in their honor while swinging their tankards high, they all of them wanted the same thing. All of them.

Too many nights in these last six months had Aelfwynn been forced to wield the only weapon she held in the face of those men who imagined they could take what she did not offer. Her unassailable piety set against their lust.

Let us pray, sir, she had said each time, enlisting the priests to aid her when she could—though priests, however dear to the divine, suffered from the same ailment as those who would have pressed Aelfwynn into their passions. They were, after all, still men.

But this warrior who held her was no Christian. What would her prayers or her priests mean to him?

Aelfwynn had stayed chaste at her mother's command and had practiced that same purity after her mother's death, keeping herself safe the only way she knew. Because any man she dallied with, much less married, would have a potential claim to Mercia through her. Her uncle had said it. This Northman had implied it. Her mother had long held that if a man alive deserved to wed the daughter of the Lady of Mercia, Aethelflaed would have found him.

But she never had.

Any man who thinks he ought to be a king will prove himself a weak one, Aethelflaed had always said. *And Mercia requires strength, daughter.*

There had been so many men in the days after her mother's death, all of them fancying themselves either the new king of Mercia or the loyal noble who would deliver Mercia, with its rumblings of possible uprisings now the Lady was dead, to her uncle in return for his favor. Aethelflaed's death had come so suddenly. It had been such a shock that Aelfwynn had hardly known how she might get through the night—but that had not stopped the men.

One after the next had they come. Some had been brutish, some charming. All of them cool-eyed and glib-mouthed as they told her lies and imagined themselves sitting pretty at Tamworth, rulers of a Mercia that was once again in contention for its independence from the mighty Wessex to the south.

Edward can make all the claims he likes, one such man had said, not in a whisper, but for all of Tamworth to hear. *But he finds himself preoccupied with fighting off the Danes from all sides and his sister is no longer here to link Mercia to Wessex, is she?*

Aelfwynn had known better than to indulge in the whispers. The insinuations. Long before that very man's head had been taken from his body by Edward's own sword, she had known it was in her interest to avoid any such talk lest she meet the same fate.

Her mother had taught her to act at all times as if the tapestries could hear her words and carry them swiftly to her enemies. It was better by far to speak only words of praise and contrition, and then only to heaven. Those who sought to turn her to their plots and plans found that all they could do in her presence was pray.

It had saved her.

Do you conspire with these suitors of yours, niece? Edward had demanded when he'd first arrived in Tamworth, setting the whole of the *burh* to quaking in fear. *Do you do their bidding even now? Is it their voices you hear whispering in your ears?*

She had employed the only defense she'd ever had.

I hope I am far too deep in my prayers, Uncle, she had said, meek and humble and eyes downcast, *to notice any voice but God's.*

Too pious to notice any threat. Too holy to pay the slightest attention to all those men who had believed themselves worthy enough to take her mother's place. Or betrayed themselves as foolhardy enough to challenge her uncle, indirectly or straight on.

The Northman who held her so firmly against him was nothing like any of them.

There had been an uncomfortable ring of truth in all his words. She had felt it inside her, winding around and around like a heat. A bright fire.

She did even now, when the real truth was that Aelfwynn had no idea what was to become of her. He could do with her what he wished. She doubted not that he would.

Too well did she know she needed only to accept it.

Such was her lot in life and always had been. Aelfwynn did not fool herself into imagining that, had she lived, her mother would have taken her daughter's feelings into account had she finally determined how best to use her. Aelfwynn would not have known Aethelflaed if she had.

Daughters of great men and women were peace-weavers at best, hostages to warring families, called upon to create bonds between enemies in the form of children. Fathers married their daughters to their enemies. Daughters became wives and laid with those who might well have slain their brothers. A woman's heart was made strong and true, for too many times would it break in the course of her life. Each remaining piece had to do its part. Well had Aelfwynn comprehended her duty.

The arm around her yielded not at all. The strong chest at her back might as well have been a wall. She allowed herself a brief moment to think of the quiet life she might have led in Wilton, her days of songs and silence spent far from the demands of men. Then she let it go.

The Northman could have simply taken her as he wished, yet had not.

He alone had offered her a choice.

Would that I had the pleasure of choices agreeable to me, her mother would have said, with one of her bold laughs. *If you are presented with options, choose. Then act. That is too often the only pleasure afforded us in this life.*

He could have killed her immediately, but he had not. He could have killed her slowly where he'd found her. He had instead laid not a single finger upon her in any kind of violence.

Aelfwynn chose to see this as a blessing.

A great boon. A gift in truth, though as she knew well, there were few gifts in this world that did not come at a price.

The old nag trudged on, carrying her toward yet another uncertain future.

She did not know whether her uncle had sent his men to seize her around the next bend. Or at all. To seize her and execute her forthwith, or perhaps take their time and a dark pleasure in so foul an act. Aelfwynn had to force back a deep shudder. Could her uncle truly have condemned his sister's only child to such a fate?

She weighed the possibilities as the woods around them grew darker and more sinister on all sides. Until she was tempted to find the band of stone that held her in place as much a shield against the winter's night as a weapon he might yet use against her. And the longer they rode, the more she was forced to think that the forbidding Northman likely had it right.

The two men her uncle had bestowed upon her, she had thought when she'd seen them, had simply been how he chose to show how little he cared what became of her—so long as she disappeared as promised and did not trouble him again. She was not precious to him and he wished her to know it well. That was a good thing.

For if she held any meaning for him, he would never have sent her away. He could easily have married her off to one of the men loyal to him instead. And her mother might have planned to use Aelfwynn strategically when the time had come, as was her right, but she would never have permitted her daughter to be ill-used. Aelfwynn doubted very much that her uncle Edward would concern himself much with how any man he wed her to might treat her.

But she knew his thinking—perhaps better than she might have liked. Even the most loyal man might, upon marrying a woman who could have claimed a kingdom, imagine himself a king. And Edward did not intend to fight battles within his own territory when there were so many without.

It was entirely possible that he'd allowed her to ride off toward a new life as nothing more than a gesture, and not for her benefit. But rather for the people of Tamworth, and those in Mercia who'd had such hopes for her, who would see his willingness to install her in Wilton Abbey as an act of benevolence on Edward's part.

And then, to remove any possible threat, he need only order that she be killed out of sight and far away, where what became of her might never be known.

Aelfwynn did not tremble at the notion. Well did she know that kings did what they would. Her uncle in particular.

Edward had never made her feel anything but hollow. It was a wonder he had not taken the matter of her marriage upon himself even before her mother's death. Aelfwynn knew she was not the only one in her mother's court who had half expected it for years.

But even if the Northman had lied and no men waited ahead, it was not as if she imagined she could ride alone all the way to Wilton now her men had abandoned her. It was not a question of whether or not she would be set upon. It was only a matter of when.

Bandits, wolves, wild boar, the weather, hostile villagers. All of these could and likely would besiege her if she carried on alone. The poor old nag had barely made it this far as it was.

She kept returning to the fact that this intimidating warrior who held her so securely could easily have slain her men. And her. Shield or weapon though his heavy arm and intimidatingly large body behind her might be, he could have hurt her, yet had not.

He had not.

That he had not done any of the terrible things he could have was not exactly a mark in his favor. She understood it made him more dangerous, in some ways. Unpredictable, certainly.

But she had chosen him.

She relaxed in his hold slightly more. Only slightly.

"Everything is not a battle, Aelfwynn," came that dark voice, edged with an amusement she did not wholly comprehend. Much less how it seemed to coil within her, flame and fever.

"Spoken like a man well used to winning them," she said, though she should not have.

That was a provocation, not a prayer.

It was something about the woods. The snow against her cheeks. The chill in the air and in her bones warring with the heat that blazed from him.

All told, it made her foolhardy.

She tensed, expecting retribution. She was entirely within his grasp. He could crush her with ease and there was nothing in any direction that might stop him, not even the wolves.

"I am delighted you comprehend our stations, Lady," the Northman rumbled at her ear. "May the knowledge of who will be the victor light your path forward."

And when she started shivering then, she could not stop. Not for far too long, earning herself another taste of that dark, hot laughter that seemed to linger low in her belly.

Particularly as she let herself wonder what this man might consider a victory.

Because her mother had raised her to fight with whatever weapons she had, and Aelfwynn had done so. But it was the old woman who had been her companion in her younger years, while Aethelflaed had tended to Aelfwynn's elderly father and the demands of his court, who had taught her a different set of rules for a different kind of combat.

Your mother is a queen, child, for all she may call herself Lady in its stead, Mildrithe had said, long ago. *She concerns herself with wars that win or lose kingdoms. But most women battle on a different stage.*

I can't help it that my stitches are so sorry, Aelfwynn had protested. She'd been little more than a girl then, awkward and cross while the older woman's nimble fingers danced across fabric like light.

I am not speaking of embroidery, Mildrithe had said, pausing in her work to catch Aelfwynn's gaze. Then hold it. *These wars have no end. Men fight and die every day. And you of royal blood. If your mother is as canny as we know she is, she will barter you to win a kingdom she might otherwise have to take by force.*

Aelfwynn had been but a girl, yet she had understood her place in the world by then. Her father had already been talking of marriage contracts and how best to use her for Mercia's gain. It wasn't a question of *if* she would be married off strategically. It was only when.

Her father had always been sickly and her mother had often ruled in his stead, even while he lived. Then he had died, and Aethelflaed had turned her attention to fighting back wave after wave of these ruthless Northmen and the relentless Danes. Aelfwynn had been given a reprieve from a dutiful marriage in the form of one war after the next.

But had her mother claimed York as she'd been poised to do this past summer, and had she then found a man for her daughter who would challenge neither her own position as Lady nor her brother's rule—all of which had seemed a foregone conclusion all spring— Aelfwynn had expected her wedding would come not long thereafter.

It would not have been forced, of course. What need had Aethelflaed of using force when she had instilled in her only daughter a sense of duty instead?

And was duty used against her, its own kind of sword, so different from being claimed by the side of the road?

We must all submit to one sword or another, Mildrithe had said, fixing young Aelfwynn with a steely glare. *Yet heed me. It is within your power whether the sword cuts you in half or holds you aloft.*

If a sword cannot cut, what man would wield it? Aelfwynn had demanded, certain even then, so young and unformed, that she knew all there was to know of men and their swords. Had she not spent her childhood observing her mother's men whether she wished to or not? Day after day they practiced their wars in every forecourt of every place Aelfwynn had ever lived.

No man carries but one sword, child, Mildrithe had warned her. *The one he holds in his hand might kill you, but that is a blessing compared to the damage he might do with the other.*

Aelfwynn had lived in her mother's court her whole life. She had seen things she hadn't fully understood in alcoves around great halls, and even out in the yards. She'd seen men and women coupling and had understood only that while her mother expected her to hold fast to her own chastity, to use it as barter, she would one day be expected to surrender to those dark, urgent embraces herself. It was only a matter of time.

No matter how she might pray that it were otherwise.

Does it hurt? she had dared to ask Mildrithe when she knew her mother would not allow such impertinence.

Does it hurt when you prick your finger with a needle?

Aelfwynn had scowled down at her much-abused finger. *It does.*

The old woman's gaze had been intent.

Aelfwynn remembered it vividly, as if it had happened only today instead of years ago. The creases in her companion's face. The set of her jaw. The compassion in her eyes.

Yet you know that when you learn how to wield it, Mildrithe had told her, *your fingers sing instead of sting. Never forget this.*

Mildrithe had lived only three more winters, but Aelfwynn had done as bid. She had not forgotten. And now she could think of little else as they made their slow, steady way through the dark of the forest.

She tried to imagine that same furtive writhing she'd witnessed with this man so much like a mountain behind her. Around her.

She both could and couldn't. And either way, the attempt left her breathless.

"You know my name. Will I know yours?" she asked then.

Because if she was riding to her death, as she must assume she was, she wanted to know who it was would dispatch her from the earth. As if that would make it…an act of valor, somehow, to submit to such a fate.

"I am Thorbrand," came the deep voice behind her.

Thorbrand.

It was only a name, she told herself. It should not have quaked within her.

He rode on and on, though surely he could not see any better than she could. The snow thickened. The air grew colder. Aelfwynn knew that if she'd set off on her own, even unmolested, she could not have made it far in this weather. And what would have become of her? She feared she would have frozen to death by the side of the road.

As they continued to ride through the pitiless wood, she still feared it.

But just as she had begun to despair, she saw a hint of light, flickering through the trees. Aelfwynn held her breath. Yet Thorbrand galloped toward the light, his strong thighs gripping the nag and urging her forward.

Aelfwynn's half-formed thought that they'd overtaken her own men, or come across bandits, fell away. And, as frozen through as she felt, she found herself wishing that the ride had taken longer. That whatever awaited her could be put off a while yet.

Just a while yet.

But it was not to be.

Thorbrand rode into a clearing, surrounded

on three sides by trees and on the fourth, a rocky outcropping that rose like the side of a castle. He dismounted with powerful ease and it took all of Aelfwynn's rapidly dwindling courage to stay seated on the horse without the great wall of him behind her. Without all of that heat and strength she should not have found comforting in the least.

And more, not to react to the sight before her.

It took her a moment to adjust to the light of the fire. When she did, she beheld two men as huge as Thorbrand. Both of them obviously warriors. And Northmen like him. One was as dark as Thorbrand, with eyes like ice and a scar across his cheek. The other was fair with red hair in braids, his gaze pitiless.

She had been afraid out there in the road. But this was worse. This wasn't a story she told herself about what *might* happen. What *could* befall her.

This was Aelfwynn all alone in a winter wood with three Northmen who towered there like mountains.

She looked wildly around the clearing, as if the fire they'd made or the few shelters that stood near the fire, linen tents stretched over wooden poles stuck into the ground, were sufficient evidence that they were human. When surely they must be monsters, to be so large and terrifying. Would that save her if they all planned to use her as men used their slaves?

Women must endure, Mildrithe had told her long ago. A sentiment Aelfwynn's mother had echoed in her own way. But it was Mildrithe who had spoken plainly of these things. *Men die quickly. Women live, and the ballads will not tell you this, but it is a harder path.*

Aelfwynn had not understood those words until this night.

Any kingdom can be taken, her mother had always warned her. *Any queen can become a slave. A wise woman imagines how she will survive long before she is called upon to do so.*

Aelfwynn understood then, as Thorbrand turned back to look at her with those dark eyes of his relentless and far too knowing, that her imagination had in no way been sufficient.

He kept his gaze trained on hers. Then he slid his hands around her waist, his grip battle-roughened and strong. He lifted her as if she weighed as much as a cup he might hold aloft during a night's drinking. Still he watched her, intent and demanding, as he took her from the back of her horse to set her on the frigid ground before him.

"Can you stand unassisted?" His voice was that dark rumble that she could feel within her though her back was no longer pressed tight to him. It was darker than the night all around or the way his men watched her.

"Th... Thank you," she managed to stammer out, though she knew not how to answer his query, for her legs seemed unequal to the task of holding her upright.

She forgot about the cold. The snow that had made it past her headdress and had turned to trickling cold, wet tendrils down her neck. She should have been blue with the chill. Yet instead she felt overwarm, as if she'd been stuck too close to the fire all this time instead of riding through this lonely wood to the mournful sounds of the wolves in the distance.

Something in his gaze shifted, and that hard mouth of his crooked, but slightly.

Why should that dance in her like flame?

"Lady Aelfwynn," he said, turning her to face the men who stood by the fire, both of them staring at her with faces like the stone that rose behind them, "may I present Ulfric and Leif, who are both kin and sword brothers to me?"

She did not miss the mocking tone he used. As if they were standing about in her uncle's court, rather than out here in all this wilderness, where the truth of who she was could only be a weapon used against her.

But then, she had her own weapons.

"Be you well," she greeted them prettily and properly, with a demure smile to match. "I am bound to trust in your honor as I have your kinsman's, who has carried me here without harm. For it is said no one can have too many friends. Is that not so?"

Chapter Four

Kemst þó hægt fari.

You will reach your destination, even though you travel slowly.

—Old Norse saying

Thorbrand took no small pleasure in Aelfwynn's clever boldness. Well did he like that she could think quickly and better still, soften what he would have seen as an unacceptable challenge from a man. Even if this was too like the courtly games he despised, it intrigued him that she could play them with such ease.

Well too did he like the reaction from his kin. Ulfric eyed her with a new interest, as if she were a riddle he was not best pleased to solve. Or perhaps as if he was trying to see how it could be possible that a wispy Saxon princess could have dared to address them thus. Leif's reaction was similar, though Thorbrand could see at once that his cousin—who only this morning had pounded him on the back and given Thorbrand his condolences for the duty he was bound to perform for their king—was considering the matter in a different light. She was that comely.

Thorbrand had spent the long ride into the woods astonished by his body's response to the woman he'd held before him. The snow had fallen all around them, yet she had been warm in his arms. His cock ached still from the press of her soft flesh against him. And as he watched, instead of lifting up her chin or in any way signaling some measure of the defiance he had heard in her words, Aelfwynn instead lowered her gaze and looked nothing but meek.

Was she meek in truth? Or was she bold as she sometimes acted? How was it she seemed to be both at once? Thorbrand could not recall ever having found a woman hard to comprehend before. He should not have permitted it in this woman who was his captive.

Yet he only stood as he was and let his

brother and cousin look long at this Mercian lady they would be duty bound to call their kin soon enough. He knew not if he was testing them—or her.

"Does a woman question a man's honor where you come from?" Ulfric asked her, his voice a low rasp to match the scowl that never left him. Not since the concubine slave he'd bought when they were last in Dublin had marked his face with his own blade, then run off.

"I would never dream of such a question," Aelfwynn murmured. "I meant only to commend you."

"A pretty answer," Leif said, his gaze moving over Aelfwynn's graceful form in a manner Thorbrand found he did not like. He did not lower himself to glare at his cousin, gods knew, but he misliked that he had the urge to not only glare but follow up with a fist. Was he a callow boy?

For his part, Ulfric only made a low noise that sounded like disapproval.

Thorbrand ignored his brother. He turned Aelfwynn away from the pair of them and brought her closer to the fire. It was built on earth cleared of snow beneath one of the trees.

When he looked up to check out of habit, he saw the branches above had been rightly rid of any snow buildup so as not to tumble down and douse the flames. Better still, the snow itself had stopped falling.

High above, the stars were beginning to come out, the gods reminding Thorbrand that his course was true.

"Warm yourself," he ordered his captive gruffly. "We stop here tonight."

He thought she might protest, but she made no sound. Only moved, the picture of obedience, to stand near the fire. He could see the way her lashes fluttered there against her cheeks, soot and shadow. He could see the line of her jaw, reddened from the cold wind—or perhaps for other reasons. Her fur-trimmed cloak billowed out, still glistening with the leftover traces of the snow, like she was made of stars herself.

It was harder for Thorbrand to leave her there and join his kin near the horses than he chose to admit to himself.

"The captive does not look ill-treated," Ulfric said in Irish as he stripped Aelfwynn's pouches from the old nag and heaved them in Thorbrand's direction. Thorbrand caught them easily, testing their weight, then hung them over his shoulder. "Or anything but resigned to her fate. Did she embrace her new future so easily?"

They had learned Irish in their childhood in Dublin and found it useful when they wished to speak freely around these Saxons, whose native tongue had grown tangled with that of the invading Danes and Norse since Lindisfarne—allowing them to understand each other better than many might like in these times of border disputes and territories forever claimed and taken, lost and won. Thorbrand watched her closely to see if she reacted. But all Aelfwynn did was hold her hands to the fire and stand as close to the flames as she could, letting the snow melt off her cloak and hood.

"You look at your ease too, cousin," Leif observed. He laughed. "Was it a battle or a nap?"

"I did not so much as draw my sword, yet her uncle's men abandoned her." Thorbrand forced himself to look away from the lady by the fire. "It was as we thought."

Their Tamworth spies had kept them well-versed on Aelfwynn's movements and once her wretched King Edward had made his wishes known, all they'd needed to do was wait. They had seen ten men leave a day before, riding out hard. Leif had followed them to their position on the road and had doubled back, talking of an ambush.

Then they'd followed Aelfwynn's own progress early this morn, her men none the wiser. They had ridden like shadows through the trees, pacing the small procession and then passing them. They had found a defensible place to camp, far from the road. Then Thorbrand had gone to face his duty at long last.

He still could not entirely believe it had been that easy.

Cowards, he thought in disgust.

"Do we teach those men a lesson?" Ulfric asked. "It is unlikely they have gone far. The next village along the road, I'd wager, assuming they outran the wolves. And the soldiers who wait even now to ambush the lady—surely they would enjoy a taste of our steel?"

Thorbrand knew well that his brother wanted nothing more than to swing his sword. The more blood, the better. It was part of what made him the fearsome warrior he was. Ulfric dreamed not of peace, but a battle never-

ending until the Valkyries came to claim him.
But he shook his head. "They must all explain
themselves to their king, and I do not envy
them the attempt. They do not deserve the
side of your sword."

The other men both grunted an assent. Ulfric's the more grudging.

"Have you told her what awaits?" Leif
asked.

Thorbrand shrugged. "She will know in
time. Better, I think, to allow her to worry
over her fate as she will."

"Christians worry well indeed," Ulfric said
darkly. "Lamentations worthy of a lyre."

And then, aware that he was grinning,
Thorbrand went to take his place beside her
at the fire. Ulfric melted off into the trees to
take the first watch. Leif took charge of the
horses, leaving Thorbrand to take stock of his
captive.

"Come," he said gruffly. "You will sit and
break your fast. The road is long, both behind
you and ahead."

Aelfwynn's eyes flashed to his, her cheeks
looking redder still than before. Though from
cold or not, he could not tell. He led her to
his tent, then watched as she hurried to seat

herself in the opening, half on and half off the furs he'd piled inside. Lest she suffer his hands upon her, he would warrant.

She amused him. He was tempted to think it a trickery on her part, but he doubted she knew it. Far too busy was she in the contemplation of the fire, staring fiercely at the flames as if she thought them alive.

He took her pouches from his shoulder and set them at her feet. To Thorbrand's surprise, she smiled.

"I thank you," she said, in that serene voice of hers that seemed to fill up the dark, cold night as surely as the fire shed light and heat. "I did not bring much with me, for what need could a nun have for worldly goods? But those pouches are all I have, nonetheless."

She reached out a hand to touch the bag nearest her, a wistful expression on her face. Thorbrand found it tugged at him. It made him…want things he could not name.

But there were more practical matters to consider this night than nameless *wantings*.

He squatted down, reaching into his tent to pull out his own pouch with the easy, portable food he always took on journeys. Particularly while traveling at sea, or, like tonight, through an inhospitable winter with no time to hunt and a high chance of failure even if he tried. He took out a portion of the smoked meat, salted fish, and hard cheese he'd packed, then offered it to Aelfwynn. She hesitated only a moment before she took it.

Because whatever else she was, he suspected she was far wiser than he'd expected.

And he ignored the way that seemed to tilt through him.

Thorbrand settled down beside her, taking up perhaps more room than necessary in the mouth of the tent. First she stiffened beside him. Then, gradually, as he did naught but eat and keep his eyes trained on the fire, she began to breathe normally again. After some time, she began to eat the food he'd given her.

It made an odd sensation move in him, not so simple as a hard cock and a draught of lust. Thorbrand knew what to do with those.

"Where are you taking me?" she asked softly when she finished eating.

He did not look at her. "North."

She shifted as if she meant to speak, yet did not. He wondered if this might be when she brought forth her womanly tears, but a glance proved she only gazed into the fire as he did.

And though his cloak and hers touched and tangled, his thigh very nearly brushing against hers, she did not recoil.

But then, she had felt his touch as they rode, more slowly than he had ever ridden in his life. Each step of the old nag a torment as much as a temptation.

Thorbrand had never set out to gentle a woman. Such a game never interested him. He preferred his women bold and lusty, with strong thighs to cradle him and large breasts to bury his face in. He liked his pleasure as loud as it was long.

Yet the woman beside him was no tavern *hōra*.

She sat as she had stood, all grace and fragility. When he'd given her a portion of his food, his hands had seemed twice the size of hers. And yet despite how slight she seemed, she had not quailed before him. She had not fainted. He did not think she had let so much as a single tear escape.

This Mercian princess pleased him, and well did he know the folly of it. It mattered not if she pleased nor repulsed him, for the end would be the same. She was his—until such time Ragnall had use for her. Such was his duty and his duty was his true pleasure. More, it was all he had. Bare was the back of a brotherless man, as the saying went.

He let the power of the fire move in him. It could be any night, any fire, any stretch of this cold land. He had spent his life dreaming of longhouses while he waited at campfires, with battles both behind him and ahead. And yet, cooped up in those same longhouses, he dreamed of fires in the open air. A dark night in a darker wood, the thick of it pressing in, giving cover to enemies and animals alike.

But he knew Ulfric was out there, eyes sharp and sword ready.

Aelfwynn finished her meal, but did not speak. Nor pull her gaze away from the flames. Thorbrand sat a while longer, until he became aware that she was trembling.

"Your cloak is wet," he said gruffly "Remove it."

Her gaze was startled as she looked toward him, then away. "I thank you, but I am well."

"What good will you be to me if you are frozen through?"

And again, she did not wilt before him, though his voice was blunt. He found he studied her with new eyes. For if her sometime meekness was a mask, that meant she wore it with purpose. Was the daughter of the Lady of Mercia only pretending to be weak? Had the rumors about her been entirely false all along?

It intrigued him to imagine that the useless creature he had expected she was might have been naught but a ploy all along. Because that meant that there was far more to Aelfwynn of Mercia than it seemed.

Thorbrand liked that very much.

He moved further into the tent and then waited. He watched, once again, the rigid line of her back as she sat there, half in and half out. Holding herself still. Staring at he knew not what.

But he was well trained in the art of waiting.

He did not ask her to remove her cloak again. Or to join him within. Yet he saw the moment she chose to obey him. The way her shoulders shook and, for a moment, almost seemed to collapse. But then in the next breath, she turned and crawled toward him, into the embrace of his furs.

Then she knelt before him, and he was glad of the firelight that penetrated inside so he could see how gold those eyes of hers were. Wide now, no small part wary, she beheld him.

Thorbrand wondered idly what she saw.

Whatever it was, she reached up, slowly, and unfastened her cloak. Then, with a great delicacy that was out of place in a tent in the woods, she set it aside.

He could see her better now. Without the bulk and fur trim of the thick cloak, or the hood over her head. Her ivory headdress looked damp, especially in the front. He reached up from where he sprawled beside her to tug on the pin that held it fast. A pin that would have told him who she was, with its fine metal and jewels, if he had not already known. "This too."

She swallowed, hard. He understood she did not wish to expose herself to him, yet it only made him wish to see her all the more. Thorbrand could have assured her that she would come to no harm, no matter what pleasures they might indulge in this night. He could have eased her worry and assured her he was not interested in hurting her.

He could not have said why he did not do so.

Perhaps he wished to see what she would do. When he was the only safety on offer.

But again, Aelfwynn did not argue. She slowly unwrapped the fabric from her head, revealing hair an impossible shade of gold. It was more like sunlight, braided in a circle at the crown of her head.

It was the dark of winter, far from any hope of summer or even a thaw. And yet, for a moment, Thorbrand looked at her and forgot.

He thought she could make a man forget anything.

But he did not intend to succumb to such witchery.

"Take off anything else that is wet or cold, Aelfwynn," he directed her, more sternly than before. "Unless you wish to bring yourself to harm. It will disappoint you that I have no intention of leaving you behind, whether the cold takes you or does not."

Her golden gaze gleamed. "You are naught but good and merciful."

And he had never wanted to get his mouth on a woman more, to taste that cool tone that made her words a neat thrust of a dagger. Such a pretty little sting.

Mutely, Aelfwynn unwrapped the bindings around her ankles and took the shoes from her feet. When she was finished, Thorbrand shrugged out of his own cloak and hung it across the opening, the better to block what light penetrated the linen flap. Then he took her wet things and hung each bit of fabric there too, so the fire could warm it through the night.

When he turned back to face her, she was still in the same place he'd left her. And now, with only the faint glow of the firelight falling over her from outside, he could see not only how truly lovely she was, but the truth of her royal blood, though her garments were not ornate. They were simple, yet fine. And the necklaces she wore were far beyond the reach of any common woman.

All this and she was his.

He could not wait to do his duty in full.

Thorbrand stripped off his own wet layers and went about adding them to what hung, leaving them in the dark of the tent together. He left on only the wool shirt and leggings he wore next to his skin in cold weather.

And as he shed his garments and moved

around the small tent, Aelfwynn followed his every move with those wide, gold eyes.

Thorbrand knew enough of women to know that the way she watched him had less to do with fear than with longing. Her gaze dropped to his chest. Then lower.

When her gaze jerked back up to his, she looked scandalized. Whereas he was almost painfully hard.

"You may thank me, Aelfwynn, for saving you from a life of dreary toil and endless prayer." He enjoyed the way his voice made her shiver, and the fact she clearly tried to hide it—yet couldn't. The way her lips parted slightly and made him long to lick his way within. She would taste of honey. He knew it. "I do not think you are well suited to it."

"You mistake the matter," she said softly, though she couldn't seem to keep from dropping her gaze again. "Had the choice been mine, I would have given myself to God long since."

He stretched out beside her, amused, and watched her color rise. "What can possibly be the appeal?"

"Peace," Aelfwynn said at once, her voice quiet.

He told himself that she had been too sheltered to know what war really was. That the peace she claimed she wanted bore no resemblance to the shameful dreams he'd had of the same.

Even so, that she should say the word that haunted him made his bones ache.

It was the December cold, he assured himself.

"Yet I have seen your monasteries," he said. He had sacked a few, though he did not deem it necessary to share that fact with her now, lest she take it ill. "Bells forever ringing out the hours. Roman words and mortification of flesh. I would not call that peaceful."

"Every day is the same," she said, and the wistful look he'd seen earlier was there again, and it was different from the meekness she took on and off as it suited her. It made him remember happier days, and the songs his mother had sung as she worked. He set his teeth against it. "The nuns do their work, they eat and they sleep, and above all they pray. It is a simple, worthy life. There is no traveling around, trailing after the royal court, forever at the whim of whatever word last reached a king's ear. There is order and rhythm."

Thorbrand laughed at that. "There is no safety behind abbey walls, Aelfwynn. Only a tale told of safety, easily breached by any warrior who dares. And what do you imagine your order of women could do to protect you?"

"They would grant me peace enough to face what comes with equanimity, I dare hope."

And there it was again, that bold gaze of hers, the gold challenging him. Enticing him. Tempting him almost beyond control.

Better still, washing away that wistfulness that disarmed him.

"Do you think, truly, that you can hide behind your prayers and yet hold off an army?" he asked.

"I cannot answer you," she replied, bowing her head and concealing the look in her eyes. As if she knew too well what he might see there. "The walls of the abbey I intended to hide behind are lost to me now. Is that not so?"

"It is not your fate to serve your god as a holy woman, Aelfwynn." He wanted to reach for her, to tumble her down into his furs and show her far better ways she could serve, but he did not. He wanted her to look upon him favorably and perhaps even do the choosing, though he found it hard now, with her scent all around him, to remember why he'd decided that was the smarter path. It had made more sense out there in the woods than it did now, when she was in far fewer clothes. "Though this may distress you, I promise you, there will be pleasures enough to make up for it."

Thorbrand had always wanted sons, as any man must. He'd given great thought to those sons and how he would raise them, warriors all, to distinguish themselves in battle. But he had thought little of the wife he might take to make those sons. To carry on his name and sing it down through the seasons long after he fell.

But this woman's combination of strength and softness had made him think of his mother and her many sacrifices—including her last. How his mother had worried when his father was away, for there was always a battle waiting and no telling if a warrior would return from combat. How she tended to his wounds when he did return, battered and grim. How she had mourned the deaths of her two eldest sons, Thorbrand's fallen older brothers, who had gone on one raid or another as so many did and like too many of their people, had never come back.

He realized now that he had spent his time thinking of the glorious death he would win in battle, not those left behind.

Not the wife who would have to tell his sons who he was while he was away, again and again, serving his king.

Tonight, he found himself far more interested in the *wife* part of the story than he ever had been before.

Especially as Aelfwynn started to breathe a little heavier. Her lips trembled. And even so, she kept that bold, direct gaze of hers on him.

As if she would only allow herself so much fear.

He was not sure he liked how much she intrigued him.

"If you intend to beat me," she declared then, "I wish you would get on with it. Waiting for it is, I think, worse."

"Waiting is not worse," he corrected her, and laughed. "I did not plan to beat you this eve. Does that disappoint you?"

"I only wish to know what I might expect."

"You are mine, Aelfwynn. To do with as I wish. Expect that."

He enjoyed the flush that went all over her then, the way her fingers twisted together, and not, he thought, in agitation.

Aelfwynn did not appear to breathe, then. "Am I to be your…?"

But she did not finish. And he found himself taut, wishing to know what she imagined was happening here. What word she might choose. Slave? Concubine?

She looked down at her hands instead, her fingers linked tightly together.

"Do not fear," he said, as if he could not help himself. Perhaps he truly could not. "When you obey me, I will reward you."

"Reward?" she echoed.

He moved then, hooking the nape of her neck with his palm and toppling her to him. She offered no defense. She sprawled out over his chest, letting out a faint, soft sound that made him grit his teeth to keep from freeing his cock and taking what he wanted.

There. Then.

Without regard to her feelings.

Her lips hovered close to his, and her warm scent gripped him like a fist, mixing with the fresh smell of snow and the wood smoke outside the tent.

She smelled how she would taste, sweet like honey. Everything about her was sweet— even the startled look in her gold eyes. Even the way she melted against him, as if it did not occur to her to do otherwise.

And though he was no less hard and ready, something in him stilled.

"You are an innocent," he managed to say.

And though it was dark, there in his furs, he could see her face clearly enough. He saw her swallow, hard. Then she nodded.

His hand still covered the soft nape of her neck. He could feel the heat of her skin, and the rough silk of her flaxen hair. Her breath came in small pants he wanted to cover with his mouth.

The word *his* was like a pulse in him.

Mine, he thought, like a growl.

He had never prized an untried woman before. He would have said he did not—he had little enough time to enjoy himself as it was. Why spend it tutoring a virgin in how best to please him? But there was something about Aelfwynn. There was something about *her* innocence that rocked through him.

He wanted to claim her as his in every way possible. This he knew.

And he would do so.

But he was a damaged, ruined man, like all men were who made battlefields their homes. He knew naught but war and his hands were bloody more often than they were clean. How could he touch a creature like this, all sunshine and honey? Surely he would do nothing but harm.

And he did not intend to harm her.

For purely selfish reasons, he assured himself, because it was better for him that she acquiesce than fight—but still. Her innocence seemed like more sweetness, more light, in the middle of this dark night. When Thorbrand had expected her to be as corrupt as any other woman too long at court. Any court.

He would need to tread carefully here. A man who rushed too heedlessly into relations with a woman he intended to keep always paid for his haste. Sooner or later.

His mother had taught him that.

"You had best sleep," he told her. He tugged Aelfwynn to him, so that she was tucked against his chest. He wrapped his arms around her and waited while she trembled. When her trembling eased, she let out a long sigh.

And Thorbrand held her there, pressing his chin to the top of her head.

Then lay awake while she settled, the tension slowly leaving her. Until she melted against him and burrowed closer, using him for heat.

He held her until he heard the low whistle outside that told him it was his turn to take the watch.

Thorbrand dressed quickly, then left her bundled in his furs and fast asleep. And welcomed the slap of the cold outside, because it reminded him who he was.

What he was doing here in this lonely wood, with the daughter of the enemy.

And sweetness had nothing to do with it.

Chapter Five

❧

*Wif sceal leohtmod wesan rune healdan,
rumheort beon.*

A woman should be cheerful, keep secrets,
and have a generous heart.

—Maxims I, *The Exeter Book*,
translated by Eleanor Parker

When Aelfwynn woke, she was alone.

She sat up, looking around wildly as if there was room for a very large man to hide in a small tent, but she truly was alone. Save for the way her heart drummed in her chest, with such violence she had to take a moment. She laid her hand over her heart. She wrestled her breath under control. And she also checked to make sure that all her garments were where she had left them. Her knife still strapped to her thigh. Her hose still in its place.

Her virtue dented, perhaps, but still intact.

Though she doubted that a woman could sleep through a man like Thorbrand's attentions. Even if she had heard the women talking indiscreetly amongst themselves her whole life, many claiming archly they did just that when their men took their pleasure. Aelfwynn had never been able to make sense of the couplings she'd half seen set against the stories the women told over spindle and thread. And now, having spent this indecent night with Thorbrand, she understood even less.

Why had he asked her if she was innocent? Why had he held her there, sprawled over him for what seemed to her like a lifetime, before he pulled her to his chest? She'd been braced for the frenzy, the writhing—but there was nothing frenzied about the way he held her to him. It was as if he were a bed to lie upon and no more. She had felt her own heartbeat, but then, to her astonishment, realized she could hear his, too.

Right there, beneath her ear.

It had seemed to Aelfwynn a rough, wondrous magic.

She hadn't meant to fall asleep, but he was so warm and the furs so soft. And she had been cold for so very long.

But now it was a new day. She could see faint hints of a gray daylight illuminating the edges of the tent, and there at the front where her garments still hung, blocking the entryway. A different sort of shudder moved through her at the sight. Aelfwynn had always imagined that should she find herself taken— though, in truth, she had never imagined a taker so large or so daunting—she would submit to her fate so gracefully as to bring the man to tears, softening the fire in him. Or better still, present herself as a willing, noble sacrifice with all the righteousness of her finest prayers.

Those who could not pick up swords and axes, those denied their chance to bear cups in halls to ease men's hearts, could do their part even so and die prettily, piously.

Aelfwynn felt rather out of sorts that she was…perfectly well this morn.

She knew not what to make of this half-taking. Or the savage, terrifying Northman who had done naught but hold her close and leave her untouched. Of all the tales she'd

heard of these barbarians, each more hor-
rific than the last, she had never heard of...
soft furs and ease.

*These must be games he plays to amuse
himself,* she assured herself.

That made far more sense. He had known
her. He had followed her. And he had taken
her because of who she was, not simply because he had encountered her on the road.
Though he had not seen fit to share his plans
with her, Aelfwynn felt certain he yet had one.

A plan he would no doubt follow as it
pleased him while keeping her in the dark,
also as it pleased him.

This calmed her, for she knew too well the
plans of men. There was no altering them,
though with soft words and smiles, a woman
could find her way along. It was a relief, she
thought, to remind herself that while Thorbrand might be a pagan beast of a man, he
was yet a man. She had handled all manner
of men. What woman had not?

She set about neatening her braid, keeping
it in its coil as best she could. Then she pulled
the lengths of fabric he'd hung the night before to her, wrapping her legs and her head
and feeling more herself as she did. Even if

she could better feel the cold now she sat up from his furs, making her fingers clumsy.

More clumsy, she amended as she pulled on her leather shoes. Her finger work had always left far too much to be desired.

But Aelfwynn had far greater worries this morn than her failures as a lady, as she discovered when she pulled her heavy cloak to her from where it blocked the entry panel into the tent and saw the three Northmen gathered around the remains of their fire, staring right at her as she was revealed.

Her mouth went dry, but her mother had not raised a coward.

Aelfwynn crawled outside, then stood with as much dignity as she could manage. There was the hint of sun, low in the trees to the east, a thin winter's light to herald the coming of another bitterly cold day. When she blew out a breath, she could see it hang in the air.

More than that she could see, all too well, what she'd missed the night before when Thorbrand had brought her here. She'd had impressions of dark hair or red, scarred face or no. But otherwise, the men he traveled with had been as good as boulders to her. Huge, massive, and not at all friendly.

This morning naught had changed, but she could also *see* them in the weak daylight. All of them. And whatever she might have thought about the heat of Thorbrand's chest, or how she might have wondered that he had not hurt her as he could have, there was no denying that she was all alone here. With *three* terrifying Northmen, not one.

Warriors all, she could see. They all sat with their heavier cloaks thrown back, so she could better view not only their tunics but their weapons. Leif, the red-haired giant, carried an axe as well as a sword. Ulfric, the dark scarred one, carried a bow in addition to his. Only Thorbrand carried a sword alone. She supposed she ought to be grateful that she could see no sign of blood on their garments. That would distinguish them, then, from her memories from a childhood spent far too near the front lines of too many battles with these giants from without. They all wore their hair long and braided back out of their way, the better to see the scowls on their faces. And they all wore beards—a practice Aelfwynn had always found distasteful.

Yet even as she thought it so, she remembered the feel of Thorbrand's beard against her head as he'd held her. And what fluttered in her then was in no way distaste.

As they all stared back at her, she found herself thinking about a woman's calling. She had been taught since birth that women were the peace-weavers, sent in to bend between the plots and plans of men forever at war. Men who could not bend and dared not try, lest it be seen as a weakness. Peace-weaving was the sacred duty of wives, or so she had been told by Mildrithe and her mother and every other woman she'd known as she grew. As such, Aelfwynn had thought a great deal about how and when she might do her duty in this way. Did not all girls? And because she knew who her parents were, who her uncle and grandfather were, Aelfwynn had always assumed that the weaving she would be called to do might well be significant. She'd taken a kind of pride in knowing the task that awaited her. Marriages were often used as truces and she knew that were she bartered off to a hostile enemy, it would be up to her to ease tensions however she could. To take no insult, even were it offered. To praise her new house and yet bring honor to her father's.

And should the peace break down despite

her efforts, mourn well her dead on both sides of the fight.

Yet it was all very well to speak of praising this and honoring that, cup-bearing and peace-weaving, but what did that actually look like?

Like this, something in her whispered darkly. Three huge, glowering men at a fire and she no larger nor more accomplished at warfare than she had ever been. *Helpless.*

When all but handed Mercia after her mother's death, Aelfwynn had done a different kind of peace-weaving. Not house to house, but Mercia to her uncle's too-powerful Wessex. She had not taken any actions that could have been misinterpreted as rising up against him, though too many had wished she would. Instead, she had waited. She had prayed almost as often as she'd pretended to pray. It had been a fraught and treacherous six months and Aelfwynn had known too well that every breath might well be her last.

Had she really thought, only yesterday as they had set out from Tamworth, that she might truly live free of that weight?

No longer need she worry about earthly kingdoms, she had told herself with great satisfaction once Tamworth was behind her. And yet here she was, faced with three sets of hostile Northman eyes, very much on this same earth.

Aelfwynn smiled as serenely as possible. "Many greetings to you all this fine morn," she said, not quite merrily. But certainly with no trace of fear.

Thorbrand indicated the pouch that he'd fed them from the night before. "The day ahead will be long. You will need your strength."

As overwhelming as Aelfwynn found Thorbrand, she found his men even more intimidating. Leif was loud, Ulfric silent. Both were tactics, she understood, as well as possible hints to their characters. The two of them watched her as they broke their fasts, their gazes hard and merciless. And Thorbrand might have been equally forbidding, but he had not hurt her when he could have. Again and again.

It was not trust. She was not so foolish. But it was enough to have her smiling in gratitude when she sat beside him and he presented her some more dried meat and slivers of hard cheese from the blade of his dagger.

"I've never spent a night in a tent in the

woods before," she observed into the cold air, the crackling fire. "It was far more pleasant than I'd been led to believe."

"Pleasant." Leif snorted.

"You must have been a captive before now, Lady Aelfwynn," Thorbrand said in that dark way of his. "You do take to it so well."

Aelfwynn chose to take pleasure in the heat of the fire in her face and the cold December morning at her back. She chose not to let the words he clearly meant as a blow harm her. "Have I been carried off on a horse to parts unknown to me before now? I have not. Yet have I been free to do as I pleased whenever the notion took my fancy? Alas, no. Or I would have found my way to the abbey long since."

"The lady was not being taken to a nunnery against her will," Thorbrand told his companions, sitting back. "She wishes for the veil. She finds the prospect of a life in servitude to her god…peaceful."

Ulfric did not smile. His eyes were too dark, his mouth too stern. "If you think a god peaceful, lady, you've never encountered one. Or his works."

But all three of them laughed at that before

she could think how to respond, lapsing into the other language they spoke. Irish, she was fairly certain, though she could recognize only the sound of it. Not the words or their meaning.

She ate the meat she'd been given as the men rose and broke down the camp, rolling up their furs and bundling up the strong sticks they'd used as poles, then securing them to three far more impressive steeds. Her own pouches were secured with Thorbrand's, then lashed to his saddle. They put out the fire, kicking fresh snow over the embers. It was only when the men started to mount their horses that she looked around for her tired old steed and found her still tethered to a tree.

"What about my horse?" she asked Thorbrand when he came to stand over her.

He frowned slightly. "That pitiable nag cannot keep up."

Then he said no more.

Aelfwynn gaped at him. "You cannot mean you will leave her here? She will be set upon by the wolves in short order. And that would be a mercy, for it would be swift. Else she will freeze, starve, and die here."

"You should count yourself lucky that you were not set upon by those same wolves,"

Thorbrand replied, his voice a warning. "Nor left tethered to a tree."

"I count myself lucky that I did not have to walk from Tamworth."

Aelfwynn knew better than this, especially when she heard the low rumble of the other men's voices. Why was she taking up for an old, tired horse? It was not as if her own life was secure—as Thorbrand had so kindly reminded her.

But she could not bring herself to back down.

"I only hope when I am old and gray I am not so easily discarded by those I faithfully served," Aelfwynn said, foolhardy to the last. "Tossed aside when inconvenient, left to die alone."

What was it about this man that made her reckless? She who had escaped unscathed from her uncle's spies. From Edward himself. She knew well how to keep her own counsel.

And yet.

She was aware of his companions nearby, watching her, but all she could see was Thorbrand. How he stood above her, blocking out the weak winter light, with the shoulders she'd laid her head upon.

Her breath caught in her throat.

"We will take her only so far as the nearest village," he said at last, his voice still a low, dangerous rumble. And a considering light in his midnight blue eyes. "But we will only do this if you grant me a favor."

"A favor?" She had not expected him to assent. If anything, she had thought he'd likely toss her up on his horse and carry her off again. Or run the poor old nag through with his sword to end the discussion. Perhaps some part of her had looked forward to proof he was a heartless monster, the better to hate him as she should, for all the good it would do her.

But a favor? A new heat seemed to flood her, scraping her throat before making its way down the center of her, until it stayed there like a flame. Insistent and low.

"What favor would you require of me?" she managed to ask.

"I will let you know," he growled. "When I claim it."

Aelfwynn nodded, mute with what she told herself was terror, though it was far too heavy, too hot. And then she had ample time to reflect on the folly of her outburst, not to mention granting such a man a *favor*. Because

Thorbrand held her before him once again, nestled between his thighs with his arm like a brand around her and his powerful chest like a fortified wall.

And he did exactly as promised. He led her old nag to the outskirts of the first village they encountered, then set her free within sight of the thatched cottages.

"The villagers here are like to treat her no better than the wolves," Leif said from his own horse, shaking his head.

"At least she has a chance," Aelfwynn replied. With more spirit than she should have, perhaps, when the red-haired giant frowned at her.

She lowered her eyes, surprised to find herself overcome with emotion. When she had never had any particular relationship with the creature. But unlike the men who had been sent with her from Tamworth, the nag had done her best.

Aelfwynn watched the old thing as she trotted away, feeling what should have been a minor loss, if a loss at all, too keenly.

"You will remember my mercy, I trust," Thorbrand rumbled at her ear. "And the favor that is mine to claim as I wish."

The heat of him blazed through her, shaking her. But the nag was gone over the hill and there was nothing Aelfwynn could do but surrender. There was never aught to do but surrender. "I gave you my word."

Then the Northmen kicked their mounts, and everything became a blur.

The day was brief and cold, but the men made the most of it. It bore no resemblance to any journey Aelfwynn had ever taken before. Not even yesterday's long, doomed ride from Tamworth. She was used to royal processions, long caravans with soldiers marching on either side, making certain that there could be no ambushes and only moving from one town along the road to the next in the course of a day. Thus had she taken her mother's body to Gloucester, so that Aethelflaed might rest with her husband secure in the light of St. Oswald, for whom the church was named.

This was nothing like any of the journeys she had taken in her time.

Yet no matter how they galloped, dodging trees at a speed that made Aelfwynn's head spin if she paid too close attention, Thorbrand held her in the same secure grip. He seemed closer to her today, because they moved fast enough that he was leaning over her, so that it seemed ofttimes that he lay flat upon her back.

She could not understand why she was not focusing on her discomfort. On the relentless cold. On the soreness between her legs from yesterday's ride that she was surprised had not woken her in the night, as she could recall from other, shorter journeys on horseback. Instead, she'd slept deep and had known nothing at all until awakening. She could not recall ever having done so before. Not in Tamworth, certainly, where she had dared not rest lest some other plot against her come to fruition while she slept, all unknowing.

It was the fear, that was all, she told herself. It had made her sleep as soundly as a child.

They rode at a relentless pace, keeping off the roads. They stopped rarely. When they did, Aelfwynn made her way behind a tree when necessary, and, for once, kept her thoughts on it to herself and her tongue mercifully still.

"You do not run," Thorbrand observed when she returned to him on one such stop, shivering beneath her cloak.

"Run?" Aelfwynn looked around, but naught had changed. There was nothing but an open field to one side that they were skirting, keeping to the trees. There was nothing else in any direction. She knew the old roads stretched from town to town, but these Northmen seem to have no need of roads. No interest in the commotion they would cause should they come within sight of a watch, more like. "Where would I run?"

"Captives run first, then worry over it later, I'd wager."

"Have you spent much time as a captive, then?"

There was her reckless tongue again. Why had it only made an appearance now? With the last man on earth she ought to test—and especially in these dire circumstances. Was she mad?

Aelfwynn knew she must be so. But she wondered, too, if she was *trying* to push him so she might finally know what to do. If he was brutish, if he was cruel—she would know her place better. She would know what came next. How to prepare herself to submit. Or to sacrifice herself, if necessary.

Though in all her girlhood imaginings of

rapturous surrender, she had never comprehended how *physical* these virtuous appeasements might become. She had imagined her pious acceptance, her hands folded in saintly conciliation…yet already she knew the feel of his chest. Those huge, iron thighs. The scrape of his beard.

The way it all made her shiver, and not from the December chill.

And she knew, then, that the heat that blazed from him, and in her, was something far different than any notion she might have held onto as a girl, regarding the things that went on between men and women. Or surely it would not wind about inside her, tighter and tighter.

He stood beside his horse, a magnificent beast that bore no resemblance to the poor, tired creature they'd left behind not long after dawn. Thorbrand rested his hand on the saddle, a look of amusement making his dark eyes gleam as he gazed down at her.

She would do well to remember that this was naught but a game to him.

"I have never been in captivity," he told her in that dark rumble of a voice that sounded like weather, not words. "I would choose death first, and happily. If taken, I would risk anything to escape it. But you have yet to try."

"I strive to find grace in all things," Aelfwynn said quietly.

Did she imagine he might find that a worthy thing? This man of brawn and power, who knew not the faintest touch of grace? For what use was grace to a warrior when he could swing a heavy sword?

He considered her for far too long, that same light in his gaze. "You take to kidnap readily, Aelfwynn."

She felt her cheeks go hot at that, though she hardly understood why. *Shame,* she told herself severely. *It is only shame that you cannot fight as others might.* As her mother would have. But shame did not explain the thick bloom of heat in her belly.

"Submission is a virtue," she told him. "You need only ask the priests."

Thorbrand laughed, a dark sound that seemed to scrape directly against that thick bloom within her, making it far hotter than before. Too hot.

"Bite your tongue," he rumbled at her, his teeth a white flash against the dark of his beard. "Submission is a weak man's sure death. And I intend to die with honor."

He swung onto the back of his horse, leaving Aelfwynn breathless and bewildered, and that before he bent and hauled her up to settle her before him yet again. Then he murmured a command to the horse and set off once more.

It took her a long while to catch her breath.

Perhaps the truth was that she never did.

She lost herself in his grip. And the reality of him that had naught to do with virtue or weakness. A force beyond any she had known. A hard cage, a man of stone, holding her fast. While beneath her, the powerful horse charged a smooth path over uneven ground, carrying her further and further away from all she knew.

But there was something in the rhythm of it. The cold against her cheeks, the furious pace made smooth as she moved with the horse beneath her, the man behind her. She felt almost sorry when the three men stopped at some mysterious signal she did not see, conferred briefly, and then, at a much more sedate pace, moved further into the woods.

Dark, scarred Ulfric disappeared into the gathering dusk. Thorbrand and the red-haired giant rode on, picking their way deeper into the forest, until they found themselves another outcropping. Only then did they dismount and without seeming to so much as glance in each other's direction, set about building the same camp as the night before.

Aelfwynn's first thought was that she ought to help. But she stopped herself. As Thorbrand had pointed out earlier, she was a captive here. Not a guest. Certainly not a bride bartered to an enemy for the express purpose of weaving peace from the ashes of old wars and bitter resentments. So instead of making herself useful, she stayed back and considered her options. She still saw no point in making a run for it. Even if she had somehow known where she was with more accuracy than, simply, *north*, and thought she could find aid, she was not mad enough to imagine she could outrun a set of Northman warriors.

She still didn't know what they wanted with her, but she could draw some conclusions. She was not dead. She was as yet unharmed. They were taking her somewhere and thus far wanted her to arrive there whole. Aelfwynn dared not put her trust in these facts, for men did ever alter their plans to suit themselves, but thus far she did not believe herself to be in mortal danger.

There were yet other dangers, she knew.

But she dared not let the fear creep in behind it as another night loomed before her.

Her mother had spoken only ill of lying beneath a man, and that man had been her husband, bound to treat with respect and care the sister of the Wessex king.

I did my duty, she had told Aelfwynn when Aelfwynn had come of age. *And hear me, daughter. You will do yours in your time as it is required. And better still, pray it take you less than ten years' time to bear your husband a child.*

Was that what Thorbrand wanted of her?

Inside her, that same too-hot flame seemed to grow higher. But there was no sense in worrying about what was to come. She could do naught to alter it. Therefore she settled herself on a cold rock and watched the men, studying what they did and how.

Thorbrand tended to the horses while Leif found a bit of earth beneath a tree with no snow covering it. He spent some time knocking what little snow remained off the branches above, then built a fire there, using something he took from his pocket that looked like flattened bark to spark and catch the logs and sticks around it.

Finished with the horses, Thorbrand put up two of the tents. Aelfwynn tried to pay attention to how he did it. The more she could learn, the more she could use. Or so she had always been taught by her mother, who had never been tender, preferring instead to admonish her daughter to pay as much attention to small things as large.

A woman never knows when the smallest, most inconsequential detail will change everything, Aethelflaed had said.

But as Thorbrand spread out the furs she knew she would rest on again tonight, she found it impossible to think of strategies. All she could think, instead, was that she had never slept the way she had last night—held close to a man. She'd hardly known what to make of it at first. Her senses had deserted her. She felt as if she'd fallen into a deep river, then let the current carry her away. There had been too much to take in. She kept thinking she ought to have been uncomfortable, for he was a hard mattress indeed, with no give or softness. His arms were as heavy as tree trunks and they'd wrapped around her so that her bodice pressed against him and, somehow, she'd felt unsteady on her feet though she had not stood.

Nothing she knew of coupling could have led her to imagine how it would feel to lie in a Northman's furs.

Even now, she trembled.

Take heart, she admonished herself. It might be another cold day darkening swiftly into another frigid night. And there was no telling what was to come. But here, now, she sat in a clearing with a fire already bright against dark and cold alike. For the moment, it was enough to sit on her rock and be glad of it.

And then Aelfwynn felt herself something other than glad when, after conferring with his companion, Thorbrand turned that dark, simmering look of his to her.

Then started toward her, everything about him so wildly intense that it made everything in her…pull tight and burn bright, like the fire.

Aelfwynn caught her breath. Low in her stomach, something cramped. But before he reached her, Ulfric rode into the clearing, a selection of game fowl over his saddle.

"How does he know where to find you?" Aelfwynn asked curiously, forgetting that she'd told herself to remain quiet. To keep her queries and her counsel.

Thorbrand turned to her again, his dark gaze unreadable. "He tracks us. How else?"

"I thought perhaps you and your men spend your days learning the secrets of these forests. When not…" She gestured at his sword, unavoidable tonight because he'd removed his cloak as he'd moved about the clearing.

He inclined his head, if slightly. "That too."

Then he closed what distance remained between them, taking her arm and lifting her from the rock. And she winced almost instantly, though not from his touch. But because the soreness in her legs nearly took her down again.

He did not release his grip on her arm. "Are you unwell?"

"I have never ridden so much nor so swiftly, that is all."

His dark eyes searched hers, then he held her away from him, looking her over as if he could see straight through the layers she wore to the truth of her beneath.

Aelfwynn could think of no reason whatever that she felt dizzy.

"You are sore." When Thorbrand's gaze rose to find hers again, there was a new heat there. Once more, it seemed connected to all those low places within her that ached and nearly cramped—sore and yet not, not like her legs—and that drumbeat in her chest besides. "Worry not. I will give you aid."

"Is that what you do here?" she asked, and she still couldn't understand why it was that she failed, repeatedly, to keep a still tongue around this man.

"I am not...*not* benevolent," came his amused reply, and that, too, made her feel so warm she almost did not need the fire.

Thorbrand drew her with him, his hand on her elbow, and sat down with her on a cold log near the flames. Then he said nothing. He only sat there, silent, while Leif dressed and cleaned the birds and Ulfric prepared his own tent for the night. He shifted at one point and she braced, expecting more of his words she should not respond to, yet feared she would—but he only drew his cloak over his shoulders.

And the less he spoke, the more the heat inside Aelfwynn grew.

"You three need not speak to each other," she found herself saying. "Yet you make your meaning known. It is uncanny."

"We grew up as one," Thorbrand said from beside her. "We were boys together, then became men. And since have fought side by side."

She dared not look at him because he was too close again. And she knew that made little sense. Aelfwynn had been pressed against him the whole of this long day. She'd slept atop him last night.

But it was a different thing to feel the force of his attention upon her. It was easier to get herself to rights with the idea of him than it was to glance to one side to find him there, much too big. Dark and forbidding, even when he appeared to be at his ease.

"I always wanted a brother, but more for my mother than for me," Aelfwynn said, as if he had asked. Why could she not stop herself? When she had kept her own counsel for so long? "What I truly wanted was a sister. I would have treasured her company."

Thorbrand laughed. And though she could see the other men across the fire, and therefore knew that they did not seem to react at all, she could yet feel their attention. A good reminder, surely, that whatever happened between her and this Northman, it would not go unnoticed.

For good or ill.

"Then I wish you better luck in it." Thorbrand laughed again. "Ulfric has been no decent company in years."

"Years," Leif rumbled in agreement. "And was but middling company before."

Ulfric muttered something in Irish that set the other two to roaring, but he otherwise appeared to pay them no mind. Too busy was he spit roasting the birds, holding them in the fire on two long sticks, his arm far steadier than the spits Aelfwynn had seen used in her mother's hall.

"How many more days do we travel?" Aelfwynn dared ask.

Thorbrand still had laughter in his face when he looked at her again, which only made her feel...shivery. She drew her cloak closer, telling herself it was the cold.

"As many as it takes," he replied.

"Is it your purpose to make your aim so mysterious that it is the not knowing that slays me?" she asked. As usual, she had not meant to speak. And she thought he might have reacted differently had her voice carried across the fire. Had she sounded challenging instead of…this softer thing that seemed somehow caught up in all the ways she ached.

He studied her in the firelight. "Why do you wish to know? What can it help?"

"Once I know, I can prepare."

"Will you indeed. What sort of preparation do you think will save you, Aelfwynn?"

"Perhaps I seek a direction for my prayers."

"Your fate is written," Thorbrand told her, his voice low enough she felt it in her bones. "Do you know it or do not, it cannot be changed."

She found herself sitting a bit straighter. "I don't believe that."

He shrugged. "What you believe or do not believe changes your fate not at all."

"I doubt you believe it either," she said, recklessly. And perhaps more loudly. "Else why would you and your people spend lifetimes battling to take what was never yours? Surely, if you were resigned to your fate, you would have stayed where you were on faraway shores and let your gods do what they will."

"That the path has already been laid out

is not leave to live as a coward," Ulfric said disapprovingly.

"You need not fear," Leif added. "It has all been decided."

She knew many thought thus, her own people included. But Aelfwynn had been raised by a woman who had never accepted fate. Aethelflaed had always fought.

Fate will do what it must, she had said. *But then, so shall I.*

"Is it fate if it is naught but sadness?" Aelfwynn asked softly.

She heard the others laugh, but all she could see was Thorbrand. His dark beard, his marvel of a mouth, his intent gaze. "Because you think you can decide your own fate, Aelfwynn? Is that it?"

Surely she should have laughed at that, yet could not.

"I decide nothing and control nothing," she replied quietly. "Save myself. And so I wonder how it is a mighty warrior believes himself without choices when he possesses more than I will ever have."

Something passed between them then, though she could not have named it. Everything within her seemed to narrow down to the beat of her heart, and the lick of flame that seemed to her both of it and because of it.

For a moment she forgot where they were. The long ride, the ache where she sat. Her unknown future, from where he might be taking her to what awaited her in his furs this night.

For a moment, she forgot her own name.

And then it returned, in a rush, in the form of Ulfric thrusting one of the roasted birds in their direction. Thorbrand took it, looking away from her as he did, and she felt as if he'd released her from the grip of his hands. She had to fight to breathe properly.

The meal itself was a quiet affair. Thorbrand cut off pieces of the roasted bird with his knife, then offered them to her. She took them gratefully, finding the meat succulent and somehow better for being both cooked hot in this cold night, and eaten outside.

But too soon, the meal was done and Thorbrand was ushering her into his tent.

Aelfwynn both wanted to obey him and wanted to fight. Instead, she only trembled. And crawled within as bidden.

He followed, quietly removing his boots at the entrance and then hanging his great cloak to seal them more fully within. It seemed smaller in the tent tonight. Aelfwynn was certain it was smaller. Closer. Thorbrand merely looked at her, and she hurried to remove her own cloak and shoes, then began unwinding the bindings on her hose. And her headdress, even though her heart fluttered.

"Lie down, Aelfwynn," he ordered her when she had finished. When she only stayed where she was, kneeling there and shaking slightly, he moved closer. And that did not make anything better. "On your back, with your legs wide."

Every tale she had ever heard of what men might do to women came back to her then, as surely as if she heard it sung before her in a hall thick with mead, fire, and song.

"But…" Her mouth was too dry. "Thorbrand…"

"Lie down," he said again, his voice a dark command.

And was not this what she had expected all along? Was it not what she had prepared for, most of her life? What all women understood was their lot, be it sooner or later?

Mildrithe's voice sounded deep within her. *It is within your power whether the sword cuts you in half or holds you aloft.*

Aelfwynn took the deepest breath she could. She gathered herself until she knew she looked nothing but calm and obliging, there in the face of Thorbrand's dark, relentless gaze.

He did not waver.

And thus she obeyed her Northman captor and lay herself out before him, like the sacrifice she had been from the start.

Chapter Six

~~~~~~

Sjaldan er ein báran stök.

There seldom is a single wave.

—Old Norse proverb

Thorbrand did not laugh, though he was sorely pressed.

Were he another man, he might have taken poorly the sight his Mercian princess presented him. For she had laid herself down before him as asked, flat on her back with her legs wide. Her arms she kept at her sides, her soft hands clenched into fists. Her eyes were not merely shut, but wrinkled with the effort of keeping them so—her whole face crumpled in on itself as if she were but braced for a blow.

Rarely had the obedience Thorbrand expected as his due entertained him so greatly.

He could have moved closer then, but he stayed where he was to well and truly draw out the moment. He watched her chest move as her breathing quickened. He saw the color that stained her face, no doubt as her imagination ran away with her.

Thorbrand let her run and run.

"I admire your obedience, Aelfwynn," he said, eventually. Then had to bite back a smile when she flinched, turned even redder, and breathed all the more heavily.

But she stopped wrinkling up her face and her eyes fluttered open, pinning him with a gleam of pure gold in the dark of the tent. "You did not present me with any other option."

"Indeed, I did not. I find your notions of captivity extraordinary. In your uncle's court, or your mother's, what generosity was accorded captives and slaves?"

Aelfwynn studied him. This time, her frown seemed genuine and not the braced anticipation of potential harm. Thorbrand found he preferred it. If she must frown.

"I think you know already," she said.

"I do." And it was only then did she appear to note that he had moved closer to her, and she startled, her gaze shooting to the hand he'd placed at her knee. "Very few choices are on offer. And yet you have already enjoyed many. I will accept your grateful protestations whenever they grace your tongue. For I am benevolent, is this not so?"

He slid his hand higher, then waited.

Aelfwynn's response was deeply satisfying. She stiffened. Her eyes flew wide. Her lips, ripe like berries, parted. She lifted up her hands as if she meant to slap at him, then wisely dropped them.

"Well done, sweeting," he murmured. And beneath his hand, beneath the gown and the hose she wore, he felt her heat rise. "Now be still."

She made a soft, half-muffled sound at that order, and he could feel her quiver beneath him. But she did not lift her hands again. She did not rock from side to side. Slowly, he reached down and pulled the gown higher, baring her legs to his view. Unwrapping her like the gift she was.

And because he could, and wished it so, he took his time.

He could hear his brother and cousin outside, talking in Irish as they sat by the fire. It was a still night, so no wind howled through the trees, disguising any possible enemy approaches. Still, he knew that they did not allow their talk to keep them from their watch.

Thorbrand had the better bargain. He was stretched out on his furs with this lovely, distressed morsel before him, far prettier than any bird on a spit.

And the more prettily she worried that lower lip of hers, the harder he got.

Yet he still took his time.

And soon enough her gown was at her middle, exposing her lower half to his gaze, covered though she still was in the hose she wore next to her skin. He laughed at the sight of the dagger she wore strapped there.

"Do you plan to do me harm?" he asked.

She looked confused until he tugged at the fabric that held the dagger fast. Then paled. "I carried that for protection on the journey. I…"

"Be still," he said again, more gruffly this time.

But he threw the dagger in its sheath toward his boots and had no intention of returning it to her.

Then he began to rub her. He ran his palms down the outside of her legs until he found her small, pale feet, and liked it when she curled her toes at his touch. He shifted around, going to kneel at her feet and then pressing his thumbs deep into the fleshy pad of each foot. And he grinned when she let out a long, low sigh.

Against her will, if he was not mistaken.

Thorbrand did not speak. He worked on both of her feet at once. Then took his time learning the shape of her calves, her knees. He took care to knead her flesh well as he worked his way higher and higher.

It would be better if she were naked, but he found he did not trust himself to take this lesson only as far as he wished to go this night if faced with the temptation of her bare flesh. Not when he had decided, after last night and the memories she'd stirred in him, that it would be better all round if he took his mother's advice—and took his time. If she was naked, he might well be lost.

For he had never felt a thirst this powerful or a need so great. And slake himself though he would, and soon, tonight was for seduction.

The plans he had for Aelfwynn would work far better were she not merely willing, but begging for his touch.

No matter who she made him remember or how stained his battle-weary hands were.

He found that the more he smoothed his palms over her legs, the more he found the places where she stiffened or moaned, the more dedicated he became to his task.

And, sorely tempted though he was, he did not slide either hand between her legs to cup the true heat of her and test her softness. Or how she might yield.

Though the need for her pulsed in him, deep and hot.

She was flushed, her eyes but half-open, and looked at him as if already thoroughly debauched.

Truly, she was a ripe bit of fruit, his Aelfwynn. Ripe and sweet.

Thorbrand stopped, his hands lightly gripping her hips. And for a long moment, he only gazed down at her, this Saxon princess who had chosen him over the uncertainty of the road. Blond hair spilling out from her braided coronet, sending silk cascading this way and that. The lovely oval of her face, flushed with a need he doubted she recognized. Better still, no more did she lie like a virgin on a slab for the local dragon, ready to feel its flames. She was pliable in his hands. Needy.

"Thorbrand..." she whispered.

"Turn over," he growled.

She blinked, then shuddered. And he was pleased indeed that his own garments were still firmly in place. For it would be far too easy to cast aside these notions of a slow seduction, plunge within her, taking her virgin's blood as his due, and then teach her how to scream his name in pleasure.

Soon enough, he cautioned himself.

A bad rower always blamed the oar. Thorbrand preferred to row well at the first and leave no room for blame. Thus did he wait, keeping his hands on her as she huffed out a breath, then set about turning over as commanded to lie there on her belly.

"Legs apart, sweeting," he said, but did not wait for her to obey. He separated her thighs himself, and then looked at the picture he'd made of lovely Aelfwynn, stretched out before him. Her elegant neck bared to his view and beyond, the graceful line of her willowy back. And best yet, the plump fruit of her bottom, presented so sweetly to his view.

Thorbrand started there, too aware of the faint keening sounds she made as he rubbed stern fingers into her protesting flesh. To say nothing of his own pounding, driving hunger.

He kept at it until she sighed, a soft sound of release. Only then did he move lower down her legs. Once again he skirted her woman's heat, filled with a dark anticipation when she squirmed, unknowingly moving as if trying to press herself into his hands.

There will be time enough for that, he promised himself as he rubbed her down. There would be time to explore her slick folds with his hands, his tongue, his teeth. To drink deep of the sweetest mead, honeyed and rich.

He had to wrestle himself to keep from doing so now, sure he could taste her already. He had to keep his mind on the simple task of easing the aches and pains her journey thus far had caused her. Because Thorbrand was going to take her innocence and bind her to him, as surely as if it were chains of iron he used instead of this. Heat. Greed. Longing so intense it would render her nothing at all but his.

Far better that he enslave her with her own flesh. That was what he had decided on the long, hard ride today. Something in him had leaped at the notion that he could take this woman who should have had nothing in common with his mother and make of her the kind of wife his mother had been to his father. Capable of raising strong sons, defending their home, and in her own, feminine way, formidable.

His long watch last night in the cold had cleared his head, thank the gods.

If he was going to remind himself of the past, better to remember the parts that mattered most. He had not protected his mother when the battle for Dublin raged. His father had lived long enough that wretched day to blame Thorbrand for her loss before going down himself.

Thorbrand had spent the years since determined to win as much glory as he could—not for himself, but to honor them both. To prove to the gods who had abandoned them that day that he was not the failure he had been at fifteen, grown into enough of a man then to know and do better than he had.

His failure would haunt him, always.

Aelfwynn was a means to an end. A demonstration of the vows he had sworn to keep, nothing more. Thorbrand would protect her and keep her, because that was what Ragnall required.

It was tempting to want more, for he could

remember well the way his mother and father had laughed together, particularly in the middle of the night when they were deep in their bed on the far side of the cottage's hearth. He remembered waking to the sound and falling asleep again in the next moment, secure in the knowledge that all was as it should be.

But Thorbrand had not been that boy in a long while.

He knew too well that this doomed world did not allow for anything like security. It chewed up such things and spit them out. *Security* was not what he would offer his little Saxon. Thorbrand knew, as she should too, that there was nothing safe beneath the sun. There was only a brief respite now and again, if a man was lucky, between wars.

Still, he would bind her to him all the same. Fate was fickle and the gods took sides as they pleased, but he knew longing. He knew greed. And he knew the task of protecting her, according to Ragnall's wishes, would be far easier if she had no wish to stray from his side.

It started here. Now. Like this.

He did not ask her to turn over again, taking care of that task himself. Then he came down beside her, stretching his body out next to hers. He took a deep pleasure in the tangle of necklaces that fell to one side. In the gown, spun of a fine wool, rucked up and her hose still visible. Thorbrand moved one palm over her thigh again, then let it wander slowly up along her side, bringing it to rest just south of her bodice.

And felt a deep male satisfaction soar in him when she let out a sigh again. Her eyes were a darker gold than he had seen them thus far, heavy lidded and not quite managing to hold fast to his.

"Tell me what you know of the pleasure a man takes in a woman," he bade her.

He watched as the heat in her eyes faded. Even beneath his hand she suddenly held herself more stiffly.

"It is a woman's duty to submit to her husband."

"Yet this prospect, I see, does not delight you."

"I only hope that my surrender pleases you," she said quietly, her lashes lowering so he could not see what truths her gaze might tell. "So you do not hurt me."

Thorbrand did not know why her words seemed to move in him so strangely. As if

they left wounds, deep and perilously close
to ugly.

"And if I cannot promise you that?" he
asked, though his fingers were restless, drawing runes upon her belly.

What he wished was to hurt those who
might think to bruise her. Not to do the bruis-
ing himself. But he did not say such a thing,
not to a woman who was his captive.

Her lashes lifted to show her gaze was
steady. "Then I shall take courage in my
prayers, take heed from the martyrs, and endure."

"Those are pretty words, Aelfwynn. What
do you know, I wonder, of true endurance?"
He could have told her of sea crossings that
had taken more lives than a battlefield. He
could have talked to her of long marches and
brutal waits, and the reward for such forbear-
ance being naught but more fighting. "What
have you endured?"

"Thus far I would venture to say my endurance spans two days held tight in a Northman's hands, no small thing."

He waited, lifting only a brow, as she
flushed a deeper shade of red. And again he
was struck by the contrasts in this woman.

The sweet, submissive innocent he had expected after her confession the night before, and yet she was still the bolder Mercian princess who could not seem to keep herself fully concealed. Her own words betrayed her.

Thorbrand could see when she recollected that his hand was even now nearly spanning her soft belly. He propped himself up on his elbow as he lay there beside her, looking down into her face as she sorted out the particular cage she found herself in.

She made a soft sound in the back of her throat. "And thankful am I indeed, Thorbrand, that you have thus far seen fit to keep those hands gentle."

And he might have decided this was a fine moment for a lesson, had he not seen shadows in all that gold he found had already made him a jealous man. He wanted more of it. He wanted her shine, not her shadows.

"There is fear in your eyes." And she pleased him when she did not cringe away from him. When she held his gaze. "I would know your fears."

"So that you may become them?"

He increased, very slightly, the pressure of his hand against her belly. "If you do not already fear me, sweeting, then the rumors I have heard about you must be true. You must be dim indeed, ill-suited and ill-prepared not only for the challenges you faced as your mother's daughter, but for any life at all not simple and disciplined, like your abbey."

Her chin lifted at that, but his words chased away the shadows in her gaze. And if they stung her, he thought it still the better bargain.

And then thought to question why he cared. Why did it matter to him that this woman, his already, should…? What? Think well of him?

That might have concerned him had he gone and gotten himself a wife in the usual order of things, but his had never been a quiet life, made of ordinary things. Not since he had failed his mother. Then buried her with his father when he had been but a boy.

You are a man this day, Ragnall himself had told him, with a heavy hand on his shoulder. *And so must you sing songs of your father, and add your verses to his, so that all may know the glory that is his even now in Valhalla.*

Thorbrand had looked up to Ragnall, his father's condemnation a heavy stain on him.

He had wondered why no one could see it save him.

May it be so, he had replied, fervently.

It will be so, said Ulfric, only a winter younger, even more fiercely from beside him.

Thorbrand knew he would make it so or die in the attempt.

He had been fighting ever since. No seasons off for farming, or wedding, or communal squabbles like some. Only battle. Only blood. And he still thought it a betrayal of his parents' memory that privately, and only sometimes, he dreamed of a quiet place far from the din of another battlefield where he might use the power in his shoulders to push a plow rather than swing a blade. To build, not destroy. When he knew well what he owed them.

What he could never repay.

He would have denied this dream if asked. Indeed, he had been outraged when his king had told him what Thorbrand was to do with this Mercian captive.

You are the only one I trust to do this, Ragnall had said. The man who was, in many ways, Thorbrand's second father, so little did he recall the man whose blood he shared aside from those final moments when he had seen naught but accusation in his dying father's gaze. He remembered that in excruciating detail. *For I know that you will not only keep her safe from harm, not only will you bind her to you, but you will make certain she thrives until I have use of her.*

It will be my honor, Thorbrand had said at once, though the words scraped at his mouth.

And he deeply disliked the fact that here, in this tent of linen and furs still dangerously deep in Mercian land, he kept catching himself thinking less and less of the vows he'd made and the duty he was called to execute, and far more of the sweetness of exactly this kind of quiet.

Did he not know that these Christians frowned on such things, he would think her a witch.

Beneath his hand, Aelfwynn trembled, though her gaze stayed on his.

"Do you make me wait to hear your answer?" he asked her. "Is that wise? I told you I would know your fears."

"I am told it is painful," she said at last.

He returned his attention to her belly and the runes he painted there with his fingertip.

One. Another. Drawing protection upon her—and he told himself he did so only because her protection better served his king. And not because he could feel her fear. No matter that he could scent her arousal beneath it. "There are many things in life which can be painful. That does not mean they are always so."

Her breath was not quite even, and not entirely fearful. "What makes it one or the other?"

He met her gaze then and did not smile, somehow. "The skill of the practitioner."

Thorbrand doubted she fully grasped his meaning, but something must have impressed itself upon her, for her eyes grew wider, then darker in precisely the way he liked.

"I have seen men and women and their couplings," she said, as if she confessed a great sin. "The frenzy of it. The agony."

"Agony is one way to describe it, that is true."

She was beginning to frown, no doubt because he could not seem to keep his amusement out of his voice. "Do you deny this?"

"Not at all. For what is life without a touch of agony?"

"Of all the stories I was told, it was my

mother who was the most dead set against the practice."

"An unusual woman, your mother." It was not a compliment.

Aelfwynn considered him for a moment. "Had she been my uncle's brother, I think perhaps less would be said of the ways she was unusual and more of the ways she was powerful."

"Was she your uncle's brother, I doubt she would have spent her time filling a daughter's head with fears that could only distress her come the marriage bed." He traced another rune, *inguz*, for new beginnings and the fertile hopes of a man and wife. Not safety. He knew better than that. "Only women tell these tales of agony to untried maidens. To what end?"

She shifted beneath him, though not, he thought, in any great effort to dislodge his hand.

"I think you underestimate how prepared a woman must be," Aelfwynn said. Her gaze touched his, then dropped. "For how could a woman dedicate herself to all that is expected of her if she were not prepared? It is no easy task to weave a peace with broken thread."

"We are all of us called to do what we

must," he said softly, and wondered then if he was drawing runes upon her or if he was drawing her heat into him. It was a strange sensation. "You may not believe in fate, sweeting. But it guides us all the same. Your mother might well have taught you thus and spared you."

"My mother never found herself a prisoner," Aelfwynn retorted, with a flash of that spirit he craved. "She would have thought her name alone would spare me such a fate."

"Nothing can spare you your fate, Aelfwynn." He moved his hand, spreading more symbols across the gentle slope of her belly. "You will surrender your innocence to me. The only question is when."

She shuddered slightly, though Thorbrand could see the glaze of heat in her gaze. He could feel it beneath his palm, her body readying itself for him.

"Are these your fears, then?" he asked.

Aelfwynn was already flushed, yet turned redder with every breath. "I will confess I do not understand how the act of rutting can be so painful and yet also so laughable that some women claimed they slumber through it."

Thorbrand did not do well at biting back

his laughter then. "Again, there is the matter of skill."

"I don't understand."

He felt a strange rush of something like tenderness as she lay there, quivering beneath his touch. Yet with her chin set mutinously, though they both knew that if he decided at any moment to take what he wished, there was little she could do. He did not intend to put that to the test. For he was hungry for her, hungrier than he could ever recall being for any woman's flesh before, but it was more than that. He also wanted deeply to soothe her.

Because it was the wiser course, he assured himself.

"It is like a sword," he told her.

She let out a sharp sound of impatience. "It is always swords. Too many swords."

He laughed again. "Indeed. But surely you know that while any man can lift a sword and swing it, this does not make him a warrior. That, I am afraid, takes practice. Skill. And no little art."

"Why is it when I wish to speak about the fearful things that men do, I must always find myself instead speaking of swordplay?" she asked, sounding genuinely indignant and baffled at once.

Gods protect him, but Thorbrand…liked her.

An ill portent when the woman was Ragnall's to use, but he could not think of that now. Here.

"If you insist," he said, "I will show you."

"You don't mean…?" He could see the wariness in her gaze then. She swallowed, hard. "Is this when you shall crawl on top of me and heave at me until I weep and you are satisfied?"

Thorbrand could not say he had ever given much thought to the behavior of men. And yet if that was not a harsh condemnation of the lot of them, he knew not what could be.

"I promise you that there will be no *heaving*," he said dryly. "And more, you need not fear that I might spring the act upon you. Do not worry over the act at all. If you do not wish it, you need not even be upon your back."

And when her eyes lit up at that, Thorbrand could not decide if he felt filled with pride that he had made her look so delighted so easily. Or rather thick with shame that she had no idea what he meant, and, it was clear, no earthly notion that there was more to the pleasures men and women found between them than lying flat on her back and enduring it.

"Do you mean it?" she asked, her voice hushed, as if he had offered her pouches stuffed with gold.

"I rarely say things I do not mean." He tugged her with him as he rolled then, so that once more she fell across his chest. "Now you have crawled atop me, Aelfwynn. What danger is there now?"

Her gaze then was so bright with hope and relief, Thorbrand was shocked he didn't spread her legs wide and settle himself deep inside her, no matter that he had only just eased her saddle-sore muscles. And no matter that he had promised.

But he was a man who kept his vows, always. What use was honor if a man only worried over it when other men could see it?

He toyed with some of the blond strands that had fallen from her braid and acknowledged that he had never imagined himself the saint and martyr he clearly was this eve. Who knew that deep within him lurked a latent Christian after all? He would have to make certain to blood the appropriate sacrifices to the real gods, and soon. But for now, there was only this. There was only her.

And what he had promised Ragnall he would do.

A task that could only be the more pleasant if he awakened her slowly to all the ways she could crave him.

So he smiled, dark and needy, and liked too well the echo of his own hunger he could see in her face.

"And now, Aelfwynn," he said, and her name, too, was honey on his tongue. She was that sweet. "I think it is time at last for that favor. I will claim a kiss."

Chapter Seven

Nē sceal man tō ær forht nē tō ær fægen.

One should be neither too soon fearful nor
too soon glad.

—*The Durham Proverbs*,
translated by Eleanor Parker

Aelfwynn felt as if she no longer fit in her
own skin.

She could hardly comprehend what had
already happened in this tent. That he had
tugged her underdress up to her waist, exposing her. That he'd found her dagger and taken
it and she had offered not the faintest protest
in return. Had forgotten he'd done it, in fact,
because Thorbrand's huge, hard hands were
pressing and rolling all over her skin until her
legs no longer felt like her own.

Until she no longer felt like her own.

And Aelfwynn had never understood what *cleaving* was, though the priests thundered on about when it was permitted and when it was not. She'd never understood their dire warnings about impure thoughts and the sinful touching that must follow. But then, what she had considered touching before now was not in any way what the priests warned against.

She understood a great many new and troubling things this night.

For she had never felt so sinful as she did now. Fair to bursting with sin, suffused in too many flames to count, wrecked by one wildfire after the next. Both where his hands had touched her through her hose, over and over again, and in many places he did not.

And now this overwhelming mountain of a Northman stared up at her gravely, his dark eyes a steady provocation on hers, and wanted a kiss.

When surely he could take what he wanted whenever he pleased. She knew not why he insisted on drawing it out. Was he making it better or worse?

But she could not think of that now. Not

with the prospect of *kissing him* lighting her up from the inside out.

A soul does not truly know how to fight until she also knows how to surrender, she thought to herself now. With great piety.

For surely it was that, and not her sinfulness, that made her want nothing more than to creep up the vast expanse of his chest. To let her bosom drag against him as she did it, because there was something in the ache of it, looming like a new glory, as she moved.

He'd been toying with her hair, but as she slithered over his chest, that hand moved to hold fast one cheek. And his other hand smoothed over her bottom in a way she felt she ought to have found deeply objectionable. Yet did not.

And besides, surely it was that same magic he had already worked. It was medicinal, she was sure. *He was a healer,* she told herself solemnly. And she was no heretic that she wished—fervently—to believe it.

"I have never kissed a man before," she confessed, though she had moved enough that she had almost made it to that distractingly stern mouth of his.

This close to him, she could no longer pretend that she did not notice that for all he was huge and hard and terrifying, he was moreover beautiful. His dark hair and dark beard made her blood a shuddering thing inside her.

And his eyes, so dark and so intent upon her, made her want to cry.

A different kind of tears, she acknowledged.

"Permit me," Thorbrand murmured.

Aelfwynn was astounded. She could feel his very breath on her lips. She felt torn, deliciously, between the hard heat of his palm at her cheek, the great stone of his chest, and the swooning, spinning, glorious heat that seemed to be coming from inside her...

As slowly, almost carefully, he fit his mouth to hers.

She thought she laughed, or gasped, for it was so foreign.

Aelfwynn had never given much thought to her own lips, but well did she know their shape, their plump softness. His suited him, merciless and grave, and yet as he pressed them to hers, there was...something else. A hint of give that made that wildfire low in her belly ignite.

And there was his beard, besides, and the

prickle of those hairs against her face should have been horrible. Instead of setting her to squirming against him, as if she had been dunked in a cauldron and set to boil, something that was not, she discovered, horrible at all.

He made a low noise, a growling, humming sort of thing, and the wonder of it was that she could feel it in his mouth and hear it with her ears. And more, feel the shivering heat of it in every part of her he had touched.

Deep inside her, the fires she could not seem to keep from burning blazed high.

And then he licked her.

She pulled back in surprise and he laughed, his mouth chasing hers.

"You *licked* me," she accused him.

"Lick me back, woman," he rumbled, and then claimed her mouth again.

Her mind reeled. In all the sinful things Aelfwynn had witnessed out of the corner of her eye in too many halls to count, or with the whole of her eyes if no one was watching her too closely, she had never thought what she was witnessing was…tongues. Licking.

But Thorbrand knew what he was about. He did not wait for her to catch up to him, he merely licked his way into her mouth, and somehow, she felt the strength to meet this bizarre incursion with her own.

And she felt herself…boil over.

It was a pure shock, new sensations exploding inside of her. Every time their tongues touched it was as if she were a glowing hot iron in a smith's forge, and while surely that should have terrified her, it did not.

For, though this might shame her later, it felt too good.

Thorbrand did something with his hand, moving her head so that she was lost in a dark, twisting heat. And everything was the slide of his lips, the touch of his tongue, the way he captured her and claimed her and took her again and again.

And yet still, she knew enough to know that this was not the act itself. This would not rid her of her maidenhead. She was not in the proper position, for one thing, as she had been before—waiting for him to mount her. That was the thing her mother had warned her against, for far different reasons than her priests had. And for another, while Aelfwynn wore far fewer garments than she should have, than was at all right or proper, she wore them.

She understood something new and shocking about herself then.

If this was sin, then she was a sinner in truth, for she would have done anything to keep kissing Thorbrand forever.

Instead, his hand moved. He pulled back. Then held her apart from him when she would have tried to kiss him all the more.

"It was only a small favor, Aelfwynn," he said, mildly enough.

And she could not tell if she was distressed or angered at the dark amusement she could hear laced into his voice and could see too well in the gleaming darkness of his gaze. And the longer she gazed at him, she became aware once more that his eyes were not the monstrous black of her imagination as befit a rampaging Northman, but a dark blue midnight.

For some reason, that made her shudder all the more.

"But I wish…" Aelfwynn began, because she *yearned*. She knew not what she yearned for, perhaps, but she was certain it began with his mouth on hers yet again.

"Aelfwynn. We have been over this." He did not laugh, yet she could sense it, filling the tent all around them. "It is not what you wish. It is what I wish. And now I bid you rest. There are many days of travel ahead."

Thorbrand wrapped his arms around her as he had the night before. He settled deeper into the furs and pulled one over her, too, covering them both. And then, as though he somehow did not see that she glared at him, he merely closed his eyes.

Moments later, he began to snore.

Aelfwynn told herself she could not possibly fall asleep. That she was *altered* by what had happened here. That he might as well have reached inside her, rummaged about, and rearranged her insides. Her skin no longer fit and between her legs was a slippery ache, and she thought it possible she might have caught the fever. All of this, she knew with certainty, was his fault.

And yet he snored.

She lay there, fuming. Certain that she would remain so, glaring futilely at the hint of firelight against the entrance to the tent, until dawn.

When instead she found that when she woke, she had slept deep.

And so the journey went.

Every day the same. The men woke at dawn or before. They all broke their fast with the provisions they had brought with them for this journey, took down their camp as soon as all had eaten, and were then on their way. Aelfwynn quenched her thirst with handfuls of snow, more plentiful as they went north, every time they stopped. Better that than putting her mouth on the drinking pouch Thorbrand carried. It felt to her too much like more kissing. Leif and Ulfric took turns hunting and never returned empty-handed, though the offerings ranged from game fowl to other small forest creatures, depending on where they stopped. They rode all day, and each night, after they'd eaten, Thorbrand took her to his tent and eased away the pain of the journey.

Aelfwynn began to think of nothing at all but what occurred in the embrace of his furs. Not what lay before her. Not what she had left behind on that cold road. Only the way his hands moved over her flesh, making her... want things.

She wanted to strip herself of the under-dress and hose she always wore, because she wanted his hands on her flesh. She wanted her flesh on his. These thoughts were so shocking they truly did keep her up the first night she allowed them to take form, so certain was she that God would strike her down.

Yet she lived.

And she wanted. And could not find it in her to consider these things she wanted *impure*.

Every night, when Thorbrand had finished rubbing her down so she felt limp and pliable, like wax, he rolled her on top of him and taught her more about kissing.

Aelfwynn had seen a great many kisses in her lifetime. Formal kisses adorning her mother's hand. Or her uncle's ring. Mouths that were only a part of what touched in dark corners, one more strange, writhing sort of panic she little understood.

Now she craved it.

Sometimes Thorbrand kissed her lazily, merely toying with her, and she knew it. She could feel the way he smiled and teased her. And though she dared not ask, Aelfwynn knew he did so deliberately. He knew the fires in her. He liked to make her burn bright, stoking the flames for his entertainment. Sometimes she found herself rocking against him, because she could not seem to keep her body still, until that low laughter sounded in her ear.

Did she hate it or desire it?

Often, however, he was not lazy at all.

And better, then, did she understand the talk of swords, for surely it was a duel that both of them must lose—or win. Nothing was enough. His tongue a weapon, his hands gripping her body, while they seemed to fight to get closer and closer to the mad need that burned unchecked within her.

Still, Thorbrand always set her aside in the end, ordered her to sleep, and infuriated her by doing so with what she found to be indecent, insulting haste.

"What if I do not wish to stop?" she asked on the third night. Recklessly.

"You do not decide what happens here." His dark eyes glittered. "I do."

"But you are a Northman. Renowned the world over for taking what you want. Why…?"

But it occurred to her what it was she was asking him. What it was she wanted. Had she truly become so abandoned? In a mere three days?

Thorbrand's smile made her shiver, deep

inside. "I have no desire to make you a martyr, Aelfwynn."

And that night it took her longer to fall asleep. Because she had always imagined that these things that happened between men and women would be a sacrifice, had she not? But if the kissing was any indication, it would be nothing of the sort.

Aelfwynn found she had to think about that. And did, until his heat lulled her into her usual deep slumber.

It was on the following day that something changed. Early in the morning, only a few hours into their ride, the pace slowed. She saw the men exchanged looks, and Leif belted something out in Irish. It sounded jovial enough that it had even Ulfric near enough to a smile.

Thorbrand's men rode on ahead, Leif now singing out the kind of song better suited to halls ripe with beer than the cold December countryside.

"What has happened?" Aelfwynn asked, and as she did, it occurred to her to wonder when, exactly, she had become so comfortable sitting in the saddle like this, held in Thorbrand's arms. He ofttimes rested one of his heavy hands on her leg as if it were his own. She had long since grown used to it, and to the comfort of his broad chest at her back.

Not a sacrifice in sight, she chided herself.

"We have passed the last of the Danish settlements north of the Five Boroughs with the Danelaw none the wiser," Thorbrand told her, his voice a new kind of hard. "We are near Jorvik. And under the authority of our king."

"Jorvik?" Suddenly his hand on her thigh felt like a stone. "But I thought..."

"That Jorvik was your mother's, perhaps? Or your uncle's, in her stead?" Thorbrand laughed loud enough that Aelfwynn half expected snow to fall from the branches of the trees all around them. "What did you imagine, princess? That while you prayed over Mercia, the rest of the world waited for you?"

"Your king has taken York?"

Thorbrand's laugh was not the happy sort. "He took it this past June, as well you know. Ragnall indeed claims all of Northumbria and yet was forced to waste his time stamping out an insurrection in Jorvik, courtesy of the Christian Danes who preferred your mother's gentle touch to his."

"My mother built a *burh* a year since my

father died," Aelfwynn retorted, stung as if he had attacked her. As if she must stand as the *burhs* did, fortified strongholds to withstand the raiding Danes from the east, Northmen like Thorbrand and his vicious king, and any else who might dare. "There was no gentleness about her, as those who would raid her kingdom learned to their peril."

"So did we all learn," Thorbrand agreed, though his voice was rough. "My kin and I fought at Ragnall's side on the Isle of Man, and named him king in time, but well do all those the Irish kings expelled from Dublin remember your mother's handiwork in Chester."

Aelfwynn also remembered Chester, though she did not think it wise to tell the man who held her—who could crush her in any number of ways whenever he chose—that it was still a favorite tale sung in the halls of Mercia and Wessex. Aethelflaed, acting for Aelfwynn's father because his long illness had taken hold of him, had ridden north to face the expelled Irish Northmen who had begged for land in Chester and then had risen against the city. Aethelflaed had fought outside the gates and then had drawn back inside, luring her enemies within. To their slaughter. The people of

Chester too had aided in this victory, pouring beer from the walls and lobbing beehives to fend off the raiders.

Only a girl of seven, Aelfwynn had not gone to Chester with her mother, but it had long been one of the tales she loved best. Was it not all that her mother had been? Cunning and brave. Seemingly foolhardy only to flip around and win.

How she still missed her.

"Better, I would think, to rejoice in your people's more recent retaking of Dublin than mourn any long-ago lost battles in Chester," Aelfwynn said in as politic a manner as she could manage when the subject was, as ever, the carnage wrought all over the earth by the endless fighting.

"I have thought of little else these last two years," Thorbrand rumbled at her. His hand seemed heavier and hotter then, but he did not slow the horse who carried them. Aelfwynn counted that as her own victory. "And rejoice in full. We sailed with Ragnall to Waterford. We fought for our king's cousin Sitric at Cenn Fuait and our return to Dublin will be heralded through the ages. Only when this was done did we return to these shores and beat back Causantín mac Áeda and his Scots, though they refused to surrender. Little did it matter. On we marched to Jorvik and made it our own, no matter the machinations of your mother and her allies."

"Then you should worry little about whatever plots might have been conceived while she lived, if the city was so easily taken."

That was a mistake. She knew it when the words, brittle like the air around them, left her mouth. She knew it when she felt Thorbrand tense, if only slightly, as if he fought his own temper.

"Do not worry, sweeting," he said after some time, though his voice was a hard thing and the word he called her more a warning. "A wise man knows when to hunker down and wait for spring."

Then he spoke no more, though the threat lingered.

Aelfwynn…fretted. Well did she know that had her mother lived, York would be under her control and with it much of southern Northumbria. And perhaps she might have slain Thorbrand's king, the much-feared Ragnall. Who, with the rest of his wide-ranging and bloodthirsty family, claimed a common grandfather in Ivar the Boneless—whose bloody rampages were darker stories still sung as warnings to young Mercian men to better themselves in battle lest these savage foreigners smite them, too.

Was that where Thorbrand was taking her? To Ragnall to offer her as a token of revenge against the woman who had nearly taken what he wished to claim for himself? But her mind shied away from thoughts of Northman-held cities and their vengeful kings. For she knew only one king well, and were it true that Ragnall had claimed York already, she knew her uncle Edward would take it ill indeed.

Perhaps it was all for the best that she was not there in Mercia for him to blame.

But then, that caught at her too. For she had traveled all over with her mother. She had been to Wessex and had seen what remained of her grandfather's glory. Her mother had always claimed a great and abiding love for her brother and so she'd gone to him, then received him in turn. Yet most of Aelfwynn's life had been spent in Mercia. In Tamworth, certainly, but she had come to love also the *burhs* that stretched like jewels across the land

and yet could position Mercia—*Edward,* she corrected herself—to ward off the savage brutes east and north.

It made her heart hurt to think that it was a certainty she might never see Mercia again. For surely she was a thrall now. A slave girl for Thorbrand to use as he pleased. To share with his men, if he fancied. To sell as he wished. Or have buried with him should he fall in battle, no matter the state of her own health.

She could end up anywhere the Northmen sailed, and that lodged in her, a too-bright scar, to even imagine it. It was like losing her mother all over again.

How had she allowed herself to think of *kissing* all these days instead of the situation she found herself in?

It did her no good to think back to the summer or torture herself with what might have happened had her mother not died so suddenly. To recount her mother's victories. It aided her not at all to remember the life she had often found on the verge of tedious. Particularly in Tamworth, where her mother's court felt settled and her people therefore more interested in their game playing than when they were under siege from yet another raid.

She had already been old for a maiden, though her mother had laughed at that, for what could Aelfwynn's age matter when she herself had done as she pleased and late into her life? *My daughter comes from decent stock, I think,* Aethelflaed had said dangerously the last time a man dared mention it. *What should it matter when a daughter of mine takes her vows? A better question is what makes you think you might find favor in my eyes?*

Aelfwynn had always loved her mother, and deeply. Fiercely. But never more than in those moments when she, with a smile she did not bother to make docile, rendered the loud men all around her silent. Perhaps, she thought as they rode on through a gray day with low clouds that threatened more snow, it was only now, when there were no choices left for her to make, that she could give herself time to truly grieve.

The loss of her mother. The loss of the life she had known. The loss of *her*, for what was she now? She might have lost her head where Thorbrand was concerned, but it did not change the facts. She knew he played a game. He had ends she could not see and that he did not share with her, as all men did. It was only a question of how much that game would hurt her, in the end.

Aelfwynn did not let so much as a single tear fall. And not only because the cold wind already stung her face. She tugged the fur edge of her hood closer and kept her eyes dry, but let herself stop fighting in even the small ways she knew. Instead, while no one could see her and Thorbrand was a grim, silent force behind her who was not currently hurting her in any way, she allowed herself to simply *feel*.

She had been late to leave maidenhood, it was true. Though her mother had hailed her as a woman when first she had her monthly courses, she knew better. She was a woman here. Now. This journey out of time, swift moving into no good future. Soon enough Thorbrand would show his true intent. Soon enough, she would know what was to become of her.

But in the meantime, she breathed and did not cry and while it was no Chester, she counted herself the victor all the same.

And that night, there was a desperation in the way she kissed him back in his furs. Surging against him and shamelessly pressing her body down on his. Reaching up so she could put her hands on his hard jaw, exulting in both the feel of his flesh, the flash of his teeth, and the rough silk of his beard.

She could not have said what drove her. Grief, perhaps. Fear—but it was this particular fear she associated with Thorbrand. It did not make her want to curl up in a hole and hide. It did not make her wish she was the sort to faint. It made her want...*this*.

To throw herself into the fire and burn as hot as she could, before his true purpose became clear and he stamped out the flames.

The morning of the fifth day was different still. When she finally dressed and made her way outside, only Thorbrand waited for her at the fire. Her heart lurched in her chest.

Aelfwynn had not exactly felt comfortable in the presence of the other men. They watched too closely. Too darkly. They muttered in Irish and wanted her to know they spoke of her while they did it.

But any difference in their situation could only be to her peril.

"Do both your kinsmen hunt this morn?" she asked lightly.

"A different game entirely," Thorbrand replied.

Did she imagine the heightened intensity in his gaze?

"They are for Jorvik," he told her. "Ragnall awaits and there is much to report of Mercia's fall to Wessex. Not least how Edward treats his own kin."

Aelfwynn had never been a queen. She had not even been the Lady of Mercia her mother had been. And yet still, deep in her breast, she felt a wild surge of temper. Fury.

"You speak so easily of my enemies," she whispered.

Another mistake.

"You have no enemies," Thorbrand said softly, but she did not mistake the threat of it. "You have one concern in this life, sweeting. Me. I thought you understood."

"Forgive me," she said, after a moment, though it was possible she addressed that to her mother, not the forbidding man who watched her too closely. And though the words stuck in her throat and tears threatened, she kept going. "I forgot myself."

"You will have ample time to remember," he promised her.

And Aelfwynn could not hide her shiver.

He offered her no food to break her fast. He kicked dirt and snow over the fire, then moved with a swiftness that made her imagine, against her will, what he must be like in battle. Deadly. Fierce. He took down their tent and bundled everything up, fastening it to the saddle. Then swung himself into position, looking down at her with a kind of triumph stamped all over his face.

She didn't understand it. Just as she did not understand the reaction inside her. Did she wish to faint after all? Kneel? Anything to push out that great weight inside her, in a scream or a song, she knew not which.

There were so many things she wanted to say. So many things she dared not say.

Aelfwynn only understood that something had changed. Thorbrand had changed, while she slept unaware. Everything, even the air between them, was as a strike-a-light in the moment before a spark bloomed.

She could hardly breathe.

And she stopped trying when he rode toward her, leaned down and hauled her up to take her place before him once more.

Did she imagine he held her closer—more possessively? Or did she merely wish it so?

As he rode, the winter sun made a feeble gesture over the far hills. And had hardly breached them when he left the woods entirely and rode out to a small valley that looked to her eyes as if neither man nor beast had set foot upon it, at least not since the last snow. Thorbrand was halfway across the valley floor when she realized that he was headed for a cottage at one end. The only dwelling she could see in any direction. It was tucked slightly up the rise of the furthest hills, its back to the very place where the hill became steep. And impassable.

Her heart started to pound, in tune with the horse's hooves beneath her.

The cottage was timber and thatch, and looked desolate.

But Aelfwynn knew.

Sure enough, Thorbrand rode them straight to the door of the cottage and dismounted, swinging her down with him to set her in the untouched snow at his feet.

"Is this your home, then?" she asked him, and it was a feat worthy of a whole hall's song that she kept her voice so even and her gaze meek.

"I have no home." There was something in the way he said it that made her skin prickle. "But you and I will use this cottage to come to terms, Aelfwynn. So you may call it a home, if you wish."

She risked a look at the empty, unhappy cottage, covered in snow.

Though her heart beat so hard she could hear it in her own ears, she did not let herself wilt. Once again, she was faced with the notable difference between duties she had been so certain she'd prepared for and the stark reality of fulfilling them.

Weaving peace did not occur if things were already peaceful. How had she not understood that? If things were peaceful already it would simply be the usual, daily work of weaving that all women knew already. If it was peace she weaved, she should expect the threads to be anything but silk. Rather knotted thread requiring skill and grace.

So she smiled at him as if he had given her a long hall filled with men and gold. A dragon's hoard.

"Home it shall be, then," she said. Thinking of peace, not grief. For the past was done and there was only what she made of this. Of now. "I accept your offering, Thorbrand. With gratitude."

Chapter Eight

Blind byþ bam eagum se þe breostum ne starat.

He is blind in both eyes who does not look with the heart.

—*The Durham Proverbs*

Aelfwynn expected a lonely cottage in a distant valley to need a great deal of work in order to do more than simply provide shelter. Or...provide whatever it was Thorbrand wished it to provide here. But she could not allow herself to think on such things overmuch. It made her far too unsettled.

She braced herself as Thorbrand opened the door and looked inside, his hand on his sword as if he expected to find bandits lurking within. He inclined his head, inviting her in, and she was thus surprised to discover that when she stepped in after him there were rushes on the floor, recently changed from the looks of it. There was a bench along one wall and a small table on another. There was a hearth in the center of the single room, and when she looked up to see why it wasn't heaped with snow thanks to the usual hole in the roof that let out the smoke from the fire, she saw it had been covered over.

It dawned on her that they had not come upon this cottage by chance. That it had been…prepared for them.

Her heart set up a low, thudding sort of beat, making her bodice feel tight.

Yet she did naught but stand back as Thorbrand tossed his furs and pouches down, then reached up over the hearth to pull down the flat piece of wood that had kept the weather out. He eyed her as he put it on the floor, his gaze a dark foreboding, yet said nothing as he set about lighting the fire beneath the typical cauldron that sat raised above it.

Aelfwynn was happy enough with his silence. Grateful for it, come to that. He headed back outside, no doubt to tend to his horse and stable it in the small building she'd seen across what must have been a yard of some kind when there was less snow covering it. Lest the wild horses that roamed free come for him. And once the wooden door shut behind Thorbrand, she set about the tasks before her with something far too close to genuine pleasure.

Because it was much better than waiting to see what would happen now they were face-to-face. And alone.

She busied herself with the pot in the hearth first. She went to the door and pushed it open, the cold slapping at her. Cutting straight through her and making her wonder how it was she had ridden all this way in the midst of it.

But as soon as the thought was formed, she knew. Thorbrand. He was his own fire, and he had kept her warm. He had made her burn, too. And now there was nothing here but the wind and the lowering sky to watch over them should they turn to ash.

Aelfwynn shuddered at the notion, then made herself cast it aside.

She knew not where the nearest river was, though it could not be far. For who would build a cottage where there was no water?

She used her dress to fill the great iron pot, taking trips in and out of the cottage to heap it high with snow, for there was always a need for hot water.

By the time Thorbrand came inside, she had spread out his furs in the far corner to make a bed, and refused to acknowledge that she was in all likelihood making her own bed too. That he could do as he wished upon that bed. That he might very well spread her out below him and take from her what he liked, no matter what he might have said days before.

What she wished to acknowledge least of all was that it was a certainty that no matter what he did, she would like it. She was that sinful.

Thorbrand looked around the cottage as he came in, and Aelfwynn stopped thinking about her immortal soul and took a measure of pride in his look of surprise. As if he did not think she was capable of the smallest, most necessary tasks any woman learned in infancy. As if he truly believed she was useless, because people had said so.

She had hung up her cloak on one of the wooden pegs near the door and when she saw him hang his beside it, something funny twisted in her belly. She chose to interpret it as concern, and purely in a domestic sense.

"I would have aired the rest of your things," she told him, feeling almost shy. "But I did not wish you to think that I would go through your bags without permission."

"I would go through yours." Something dangerous glinted in Thorbrand's midnight gaze. "I have."

Aelfwynn blinked at that. But naturally he had done so. Why was she surprised?

"Are we on the same footing then?" she asked lightly. "That was not my impression."

His mouth curved and she still could not quite make sense of what happened inside her when he did that. Because she knew that mouth, now. She had tasted it. She had, more than once, had his tongue inside her own mouth—and even thinking about it made her feel red and swollen all at once.

"No, indeed," he said, his voice gone rough, "we are not."

And then there was naught but silence.

Thorbrand stood there just inside the door and Aelfwynn reflected that she had not had sufficient time to simply...gaze upon him. They were always riding on his horse. Or it was dark. Or the cold and snow made it impossible to do more than hide behind her hood. Or yet he wished to speak to her of her aptitude for captivity and it was all she could do not to let loose her own temper in return.

She was not certain she was *prepared* to gaze upon him, now that she could. Inside the cottage, his hugeness was a different beast. His shoulders seemed to fill the whole of the room. He was broader than the door behind him. He was tall enough that he had reached the roof with no difficulty. Surely he need only shrug and could touch one wall, then the other.

Aelfwynn had known full well he was a large man. Yet here he seemed all the larger.

And she could hardly recall thinking him brutish, back in that road south of Tamworth. For now all she saw was the beauty of him. Remote, undoubtably ruthless, made of stone and iron—though there was snow dusting his beard, melting into something sparkling as she watched.

He was more beautiful than any man she had ever beheld. Than all the men she had ever beheld.

She had grown accustomed to these desolate landscapes they had traveled through at such speed. Bared forests overlooking distant moors. Fields lying fallow beneath the press of darkness this close to midwinter. Stark and lonely, all of it, and in the middle of it was Thorbrand.

And he was so *alive*. He laughed loud, he rode hard, and given infinite opportunities to harm her, he had not. She knew not why, yet he had used those warrior's hands of his, battered and calloused, to rub her until she was limp. To spread fire all over her body until she wanted nothing more than to surrender to him. To give him things she knew not how to name.

Then again, perhaps that was why.

"Take heed, sweeting," he growled, though his gaze was bright. "Else I will take the invitation I see in your gaze here and now."

Aelfwynn was trembling, but she cast her eyes toward the floor and did her best to look meek instead of…aflame.

"I am weary." Yet Thorbrand did not sound in any way weary. "I have been too long on the road and I am not a Saxon content to steep in my own filth. I must bathe."

"I have heated some water." Aelfwynn

nodded toward the cauldron that had still not begun to boil, though she knew it would. "There is no tub, though it will be easy enough to wash."

"We have no need of a tub." There was a different note in his voice, then. She scarcely dared look at him now that it was only the two of them here, and he had already warned her about *invitation*, but she couldn't seem to stop herself.

Sure enough, there was a gleam in those dark blue eyes of his that made everything inside her seem to...change position.

"Come, then," he said. "I will take you to the hot springs. We will bathe together."

It was true, then, what she'd heard about these warriors from overseas and their constant bathing. Aelfwynn washed herself diligently, as she had been taught, and had looked forward to doing so here now that the woods were behind them—but she did not fully immerse her person in water any more than necessary. Mildrithe had always held that such practices brought on the *gepos* with a vengeance, and any who indulged would be lucky indeed that the illness not take root in the chest.

Though Thorbrand did not look as if he tol-

erated such petty weaknesses as a thick head
and a scratchy throat.

Aelfwynn felt hushed and humming straight
through. More, there was that look of intense
command all over his hard face. She could not
have defied him if she wanted to.

She did not want to.

Instead, she banked the fire. Then, as if in a
dream, she walked to the door where he stood
and pulled her cloak on. He did the same.
Then he led her outside into the cold, where
she found to her surprise that he had stamped
down a path through the snow from the front
door of the cottage. It was easy enough to
walk around to the back of the cottage to the
small stable where his horse nickered a greeting, then beyond it, toward the steep hill that
loomed behind. She wondered if he intended
to take her on a march up that hill, a daunting prospect, though she dared not complain.
Yet at the base of the hill's steep rise was a set
of boulders. Thorbrand led her to them, then
between them.

And when Aelfwynn stepped through the
stone gateway, she stopped. Then gasped
aloud.

For a pool waited there, hot enough that

steam rose from its surface. Though there was snow all around, dusting the surrounding boulders, it yet bubbled. And as it did, a rich, earthy scent filled the air.

Aelfwynn had never seen its like, though she had heard tell of such wonders, far to the south in Wessex.

She went to the edge and knelt down, tugging off her glove so she could skim her palm over the surface of the water. The heat was a miracle. It sank deep into her skin, like the heat of summer in this cold, dark place. She lifted her hand, bemused, to rub her fingers together for even the water itself felt different. Not simply warm. But like silk.

"I trust it meets with your approval," Thorbrand rumbled. "I know your people prefer their dirt and grime."

Aelfwynn had not precisely forgotten about him. That was impossible. But the pool had so captivated her that it shocked her a little to recall that he stood there behind her even now. She shifted where she knelt to gaze up at him, intending to gently point out the difference between diligent washing and *dirt and grime*—but her mouth went dry.

For Thorbrand was not simply standing there making remarks. He was undressing.

For a moment, Aelfwynn simply froze.

She'd seen glimpses of the male form, though she had always been too aware of those who ever watched her to see if she looked too long. And she certainly had impressions of Thorbrand's form. She had lain upon him. She'd woken, some nights, to find his broad thigh thrust between her own. She knew his mouth, and thinking so made her feel too hot, suddenly. Even hotter than the water itself.

If she was truly pious, surely she would protest. If she was pure in heart as well as body.

But no protest formed on her tongue.

It was wicked to look upon any man who was not her husband, and so she knew it must be wickedness that swelled in her as Thorbrand tossed off his cloak and set his weapons within reach of the water's edge. And then, those dark blue eyes of his meeting hers with a kind of mild challenge, he first pulled off his tunic. Then the tighter layer he wore beneath.

Aelfwynn had seen male chests, but only from a distance. Soldiers practicing in the forecourt, laborers in the fields.

But never before had a man simply stood before her, close enough to touch.

It had to be wickedness, that throbbing pulse of fire deep in her belly. That alarming slickness between her legs that she might have thought were her courses were it not the wrong time.

And then, while her mouth dropped open and she felt a kind of heat rush at the back of her eyes, Thorbrand stripped off the rest of his garments and stood before her.

Naked.

Aelfwynn could hardly accept what she was seeing. Every part of him was massive. His arms were thick with muscle. His chest, that wall she knew well pressed against her own back and beneath her cheek as she drifted into slumber, was shaped like one of the boulders that stood sentry around them and livid with the marks of his profession. Scars crisscrossed his flesh, some silvery with age and some new. And though she knew this man was naught to her but an enemy, a master whether she liked it or did not, yet she still felt her fingers tremble with the need to trace each one of them.

To taste them with the kisses he had taught her.

His thighs seemed larger than she recalled

from the nights spent in his furs. His legs were mighty and powerful. And between them, his male part stood thick and proud.

Aelfwynn had seen such parts on too many horses and cattle to mention and had thought about them not at all. Yet there was something about Thorbrand that made the wickedness inside her bubble up like the spring that must feed this pool.

There was amusement in his dark gaze again, and too something darker. He moved to the side of the pool, only glanced at her, then jumped. Aelfwynn expected a huge splash and drew back, but he hit the water cleanly. Then disappeared beneath its surface like a blade.

His blade, a voice in her whispered. *He has left you with his blade.*

His weapons were within reach. His sword looked far too heavy, but his dagger—

"You are welcome to try it, Aelfwynn," came his deep voice. She jumped, and when she looked at the pool, was not at all surprised to find him there, his head above the water. Watching her as if he had anticipated what she would do. "But know this. I disarm great warriors on battlefields with little trouble. What sport would there be in it if I were to take that dagger away from you?"

"Perhaps no sport. Yet I might leave you with a new scar to add to your collection."

"Aelfwynn. Sweeting." His grin was a better blade, then. And it sunk into her flesh, deep. "You will not be leaving me at all."

It was all too much, suddenly. All she'd lost. All that was ahead of her, each possibility bleaker than the last. And in the center of it was this man who had kissed her, night after night, making her nothing so much as *complicit*.

"I see the spark in your eyes, girl," came the rumble of his voice, though he stayed where he was, leaning back against the other side of the pool, his arms stretched out on either side, looking as if he was fully at his ease. "I admire that you think you can best me. But you must know you cannot win."

Her heart pounded. Shame, she thought. And that wickedness. They collided within her, until she could not breathe for the weight of them.

"Yet surely I must try," she whispered.

"If you must."

There was a carelessness in the way he said that. As if he was bored here.

Aelfwynn lunged for his dagger. She swept it up, noting the jewels on the hilt that spoke of his high status, but she whirled back towards the pool as quickly as she could, intending what, she knew not—

But this time, when she hit the stone wall of his chest, he was steaming from the water, slick and wet.

And more, that ruthlessness in him overtook her.

He took the dagger from her hand as if she'd offered it to him. And he didn't stop there. She had not seen him leap out of the pool, but he was there at its edge and then he was on her. It was nothing to him. She panted, yet his breath was unaffected.

And it had been a game after all, she understood. For five days he had shown her his strength in small doses, but she had not understood it.

He used it now. Aelfwynn could not move. She could not fight. He simply held her, no matter how she struggled, and did what he would.

He stripped her of her garments, one after

the next, with a ruthless efficiency. She was breathing so loud she was very near sobbing, yet he was implacable. And it took her some time to work out that he was not trying to hurt her.

Though the realization made her stomach take a funny turn and she knew not which ill humor gripped her most. She felt shame well enough as her flesh was bared to the cold air, and more because of the fearsome warrior crouched over her, relentlessly and implacably male.

But that wickedness never left her. It seemed to weave itself into that first kick of panic, then bloomed.

No good could come from naked flesh exposed, well did she know this. Yet when he finished removing all her clothing, he merely hauled her up into his arms as if she weighed no more than her own cloak. She had the impression that face of his, beautiful like stone and intent dark eyes, and she thought that were that her last sight, there could be worse—

Then she hit the water. And sank.

And it took too long to understand he'd gone and tossed her into the pool.

Aelfwynn fought for the surface, sputter-

ing, and only as she flailed for her breath
did she feel Thorbrand again. His arms went
around her as he lifted her so her head was out
of the water. Then he settled her against him
while water streamed from her eyes, her nose.
She coughed more of it out, only gradually re-
alizing she did so against his wide shoulder.

"Do you drown me?" she managed to ask.
She pushed at his chest, his shoulders, desperate—though he did not move or seem to notice. Something like a fury tore through her,
though she knew well that was only permis-
sible in a lady when it was her mother.

But you are no lady either way, a voice inside reminded her. *You are but his slave.*

"You forget yourself, Aelfwynn," came the
dark, forbidding rumble of his voice.

Then his hand was at the back of her head,
and she did not understand the tugging she
felt until her hair tumbled down around her.
He made a deep noise that seemed to wind
itself around and around inside her. Then he
raked his fingers through her braid until her
hair hung wet and free and floated where it
touched the water.

She couldn't breathe. She wanted to fight.
She wished she knew *how* to fight.

"You forget yourself," he growled again, as if he could hear her thoughts. "Let me remind you."

And then he claimed her mouth with his, and everything seemed to shatter.

Aelfwynn was aware of too many things at once. The heat of the water. The way her breasts were slick and yet ached against his bare chest, far worse than when there had been layers of wool and linen between them. He held her against him, her legs wrapped around him as if she were on a horse, and she could feel the thick shaft of him hard against her belly.

His hands sank deep into her hair, holding her head where he wished. And all the while he plundered her mouth, making it clear to her that whatever game he had played in his furs these last nights, he played no more.

And she understood this, then. That in all the years she had spent contemplating her purity, her chastity, the price of her maidenhead and what giving it away to the properly chosen husband would entail, she had always assumed that it would occur after a period of sober reflection.

But this was a storm.

She could think only that, then no more.

The water was hot, but they were hotter.
His mouth left hers, tracking down the side
of her neck and he made a deep, growling
sound that made everything in her shiver, then
sharpen.

This, then, was that frenzy. She felt it inside her. She became it.

He shifted how he held her. His hands
moved to the swell of her bottom, lifting her
so her woman's flesh found that thick shaft
of his, and then...bloomed bright.

She did not fully grasp what he was doing,
only that it sent a peculiar kind of pain shooting through her. Though did not hurt. It only
made her feel tighter, wilder.

Up and down he moved her, rubbing himself in that private furrow he seemed to know
ached beyond measure.

He muttered words against her neck, strange
words she could not understand, and yet they
seemed to arrow straight to that place where
they were not quite joined.

Slowly, then quickly, a new storm began.
It poured out from that pulsing place within
her, taking her over, until it gripped her completely.

Aelfwynn broke apart.

Distantly, she heard the dark sound of Thorbrand's laughter. The storm was inside her, someone cried out in a voice very like her own, and she was shuddering and fighting for breath.

Yet he cradled her against his chest, and then, even as she shuddered, began to work that shaft of his deep between her legs.

"Thorbrand…" she managed to get out.

Though she knew not what she pleaded for.

"It will hurt," he growled. "But heed me, Aelfwynn. You will not weep. You will not cry out. You are the daughter of queens and kings and you will suffer beautifully. For me."

Where he prodded against her it felt rude, and new. She moved her hips as if she could make it better that way. Then only realized as she did that it was…connected to this thing, the wicked knot that hummed inside her, when he hissed in a breath.

"Will I not cry out?" she asked, for the storm that had taken her away had not left her, and now it only seemed to grow,

"You will not." His voice was stern. "If you must do something, you may bite me. You may thank me for this privilege."

"Thank you," she whispered, though she

in no way felt *thankful*, but then Thorbrand smiled. His eyes, as dark as midnight, gleamed. And she felt as if she gleamed, too.

His huge hands gripped her hips and then curved around, splitting her wide.

And then he proceeded to do just that.

His gaze held hers. He did not falter. And slowly, surely, he began to work that male part of him inside her.

Inside her.

And she was so slippery, and she *ached*, and yet he pressed in, stern and steel. Surely it should not have fit, but even her untried flesh obeyed him. The pressure grew and grew, and she shuddered against it, desperately trying to move the hips he held still. She had no choice but to use parts of herself she'd never noticed before, trying to accommodate him. Trying to take him. Trying not to rip apart—

She wanted to scream that he was hurting her, but she did not dare. For it was not true.

Hurt was such a small word, and could not possibly encompass…this. How it felt to be torn apart, little by little, by the Northman who watched her as if this sundering was a joy. Until she wanted it to be so, to please him.

Then, somehow, she could feel the vast

thickness of him inside her own body, nudged up against the place where she ended. And his hips pressed so tight against her, it was as if they were one.

They were, she thought, in the next hot, half-panicked moment.

She wanted, desperately, to do something. Maybe push him off her. Maybe pull him closer. But she could not move. He held her steady and only watched as she bucked against him, moving her hips whatever scant amount the grip he had on her allowed.

"Remember what I told you," he warned her. "No sound."

A different kind of sensation seemed to be gathering from her fingers, her toes, and yet connected like a new ache to that place inside her that he filled overfull. She dropped her head to his shoulder and found her mouth open against the slick, steel expanse of his shoulder. And she found herself panting there, still wriggling her hips this way, then that, though she could not seem to avoid the bright hot heat of his male flesh that pinned her thus. No matter what she did.

She became aware again of the tight peaks of her breasts, and something about the way she dragged them against his chest connected to that heavy weight inside her. Her mouth against his skin was a part of it too, and so too the way his battle-scarred hands gripped the back of her, splitting her, making that full, deep stretch take her over.

Aelfwynn followed some instinct she did not recognize and locked her ankles together around his hips, then moved a little more.

Once, then again, she made room and yet filled herself more. The stretch became something else. And then suddenly, there was nothing in it but heat.

That sweet, glorious fire that rendered her helpless and half mad with it.

"Well done, sweeting," Thorbrand said, and she shivered as if pleasing him was a flame all its own.

And then he changed everything, pulling himself back as if leaving the clasp of her body only to slide himself back in. Then he did it again.

Then he did it harder.

"Now, Aelfwynn, you can make all the noise you like," he growled in her ear.

And so she let her head drop back, and she screamed.

Because this was a rough wonder, a slick encompassing joy. She gripped him and he gripped her in turn, and all the while his staff plunged deep.

Again and again he claimed her. When that proved too much, he gripped the back of her head and guided his mouth to hers again. Then she had his tongue and she had his hard male flesh too. Both took her, both destroyed her, and it took only a few thrusts like that before he pulled her apart all over again.

And this time, when she cried out against his lips, he sounded his own cry. She felt that great staff within her jerk, then flood her, so scalding hot the water around them felt cool.

Her final thought, as his mighty chest heaved and he held her in his arms, was that this was her ruin.

Aelfwynn, daughter of Aethelflaed and granddaughter of Alfred, was ruined.

And she could not wait to ruin herself all over again.

Chapter Nine

Verðr þat er varir ok svá hitt er eigi varir

Much happens that one expects the least.
—from *Grettis Saga*,
translated by T. Kinnes

A snowstorm rolled in that night and settled in over the valley.

Thorbrand could not say he minded. He had provisions enough, having stashed foodstuffs, basic tools, and his bow and axe here before he had headed south to take possession of his princess. He'd made certain there was wood enough to burn so he might keep the fire hot no matter how long they needed to stay here, and he and Leif and Ulfric had spent a day or two performing necessary repairs on this old cottage that the nearest villagers, several valleys away, tho[...] [...] upheaval since [...] the las[...] vik some eight y[...] to be quite so rem[...] wh[...] the [...] kept changing hand[...] and new[...] turn up at any time.

There was safety i[...] [...] But [...] brand was not much co[...]ned with s[...]ty. Not with a snowstorm batt[...] [...] the thatched roof, as effective at keepin[...] predators away as a fortress.

Giving him leave to think of nothing but Aelfwynn.

He had taken her innocence in the hot pool and he could still feel the first clasp of her body on his and the way she'd taken him deep, her woman's flesh obedient even as the rest of her had trembled at his stark possession.

For he had planned to take her, there in the pool where the hot water might wash away the stains he bore—if only for a small while. But not quite like that. He had meant to honor the sweetness he'd tasted in her on their journey.

But then she had brandished his own weapon at him, fearless and determined. His heart had pounded as if this were a battle,

, at that. His cock had been
the dagger she'd tried to wield.
all of Thorbrand's good intentions had
en lost.

Aelfwynn's beautiful surrender had only
whetted his appetite.

He had carried her from the pool, draping
only her cloak over her body as he'd delivered
her back to the cabin. He'd returned alone to
gather their things, enjoying the slap of cold
against his heated skin. It had only made him
hungry for more.

Once inside, he had found her sitting on one
of his furs by the hearth in the center of the
small cottage, combing out that flaxen hair
of hers with her fingers. He had moved her
hands out of his way as he'd gathered her onto
his lap, then done the combing himself. His
fingers were a blunter implement, certainly,
and he knew not where the urge to do it came
from, yet he indulged it all the same.

And it had built again in him, the thirst he
could not quench. Thorbrand had held her before him the way he'd held her on their long
rides. He'd moved her head to one side and
feasted on her neck, moving his palms where
they willed on her sweet flesh. He found her

breasts, plump and high, and played with them until she moaned and his cock blazed again with heat and need.

He had lifted her up and tilted her forward enough so he could sheath himself within her, then brought her against him once more, her back in a lovely arch.

You know how to ride, Aelfwynn, he had said. *I want you at a canter.*

She had shivered and flushed red, his pretty little captive. She had pulled her plump lower lip between her teeth. He'd seen the faintest hint of moisture on her brow. All for him.

Then, at first awkwardly, she had figured out how to lift herself up then sink back down, rubbing her sweet bottom against him as she moved.

Still he had played with her breasts, plucking and pinching her nipples, and grinning darkly as she had made all kinds of greedy little sounds. A quick hiss, a moan, as she had worked him, becoming wetter and softer as she moved.

To reward her for such quick learning and innate skill, Thorbrand had slid a hand down between her legs, and found the stiff bit of flesh that stood proud, there within the slick folds that gripped him with such soft heat.

Then he had played her like a lyre, a pinch to her nipple and pinch below. A dedicated strumming until he made her sing.

Then sob as she shook around him.

He had taught her how to tip forward, still sobbing out her release, and how to brace herself on her hands and knees while he gripped her hips and pounded out his own pleasure from behind.

When he found them snowed in the following morning, it seemed nothing so much as a sign from the gods.

There would be time enough once Ragnall summoned them to worry about the rest of it, he assured himself. The plot and the plan. The life they would lead until Thorbrand's king had need of the very subtle weapon that was Aelfwynn, daughter to the Lady of the Mercians—though clearly sharp-edged enough that her uncle had wanted the threat of her removed forever.

There would be time, then, to speak of the role she would play. To explain where they would go and what would be expected of her.

But first it was time he put his long nights of seduction to the test.

He did so with a passion he told himself was only because he had been forced to wait. Only because he had built up a hunger so powerful it required regular feeding to feel himself again. To even attempt to sate himself.

Thorbrand did not feel anything but Aelfwynn, day after day. And he could not have said he was any nearer to sating himself. No matter how he applied himself to the task.

They did not speak of what she was to him, or what might happen when they left this cottage. Wise woman that she was, she never asked.

And accordingly, he did not ask himself what it was he did here. Or what it meant to lose himself like this, like a man possessed instead of a man fulfilling his duties and his vows.

When he knew better than to imagine what he could never, ever have. A warm woman, a quiet home.

He told himself that he was not betraying the vows he'd taken. That he was only setting their future in stone.

And so it was, stone by stone, that they learned each other.

Thorbrand had never spent enough time with a woman to learn her thus. One night, perhaps two, had he entertained the same woman in his furs, but was always in between battles. On the road, forever moving, fighting, focusing on what lay ahead.

He could not recall a time in his life when he had not been, if not actively fighting a war, preparing for the next. For there was always a next, new war to fight. These were ages drenched in blood, as was known far and wide. Doomed seasons and petty kings led only to more blood spilled, but such was not Thorbrand's concern. His sword had been pledged to Ragnall long ago.

When he was not out on a battlefield, Thorbrand trained in battle tactics. Sometimes he was focused on recovering from what wounds he might have sustained. Always did he offer his support and counsel to his king when called upon to do so. His head was always in the next fight, the next disputed territory, the next stretch of cold land they would take, then claim, then defend.

Thorbrand spent very little time worrying

about how to take his pleasure. There were always women. There was always another mead hall. There were songs enough to sing, ancient heroes to admire and gods to praise. There was no shortage of pretty things to fill his cup and warm his furs.

But here in this cottage there was only Aelfwynn and this greedy want in him that grew ever bigger, ever sharper.

And more time than he could remember ever spending on his own, away from the king who had made the boy he'd been first into a man, then into a warrior. Much less the men he fought with and considered his brothers, whether they were closely related or not. No wars to plan. No land to defend.

Just Thorbrand and his woman and a valley filled with snow and silence.

One day bled into the next. When the snow eased, Thorbrand hunted what paltry game remained this time of year and foraged what little he could from the bleak forest and the valley below. He cared for his horse, bathed daily in the hot springs and encouraged his skeptical Saxon to do the same, and was no warrior, here. Here he was a simple man who lived off the land and took care of what was his.

Very like the dreams he'd had, little as he might wish to think about such things in the light of day. Or at all.

But what he did most was learn her.

He was obsessed with that golden hair of hers and how it caught the firelight. Some nights they never made it from the furs spread before the hearth to the pallet in the corner. She slept as hard as she ever had, but sometimes he woke her in the dark, lifting her leg high as she sprawled over his chest and finding his way inside her. She would come sleepily half-awake, her face in the crook of his neck and her mouth against his skin, while he gripped her tight and thundered them both to bliss.

Some mornings he insisted she never dress at all and go about her chores bared to his view, forever sneaking glances at him, so that by the time he caught her up and thrust himself into her, they were both at fever pitch.

She was his. In every possible way.

He taught her how to kneel before him and take him deep into her mouth. And he knew he had trained her well when, after he poured himself down her throat, she was trembling and greedy and desperate for him to put his hands between her legs and bring her to her own release in turn.

They spent time in the pool doing more than simply bathing, where he taught her any number of things in the embrace of the hot water. The pleasures of cold snow against warm flesh. How to climb him, how to grip him, and how different those things were when the water lifted her than when he held her aloft in the cottage.

The snow kept coming. As soon as one storm eased, it might seem clear for the stretch of a day only for another storm to move in.

The days passed even so. The light began to change, lasting longer before it gave way to night. It was a small thing, but still, within it was the hope of spring. With the coming of spring, Thorbrand knew, came too the promise of the sea. And the lands that waited for him in the west.

Lands he would settle with Aelfwynn at his side, a far brighter prospect now than he had initially anticipated.

But a duty made palatable was a duty all the same, surely. He told himself duty was all it was.

Today Thorbrand found himself out on a

gloomy afternoon, checking the traps he'd laid in the hope that there might be meat for his dinner tonight. Though if there was nothing he would eat the bread Aelfwynn baked each day using the stores he'd brought before and call it a feast.

No meat awaited him out in all that sullen gray, but he thought of the magic Aelfwynn could work with very little and was as pleased as if a hart had stumbled into one of his crude traps. Down at the bottom of the valley, he left the woods and walked up its center, his gaze on the cottage in the distance. He could see the smoke from the hearth stain the low sky above the thatched roof. And now and again, a flash of light from the fire when Aelfwynn opened the door as she went about her tasks.

They had not discussed *tasks*, either. She had woken their first morning, surveyed his stores with a practiced eye, then set to work.

Proving herself, he had thought then. He had expected her to fail. For what could a pampered Saxon princess know of real work? The mother had fought and toppled kings, so surely the daughter would consider herself above the menial labor of life. But she had proved him wrong. Day after day, she cooked their food and frowned severely at him should he make any attempt to do more than eat it.

She kept surprising him. It was starting to make his chest feel tight. Or maybe it was simply being here in this remote, craggy place. Away from all he knew. Tucked up with Aelfwynn in a cottage with winter still thick all around them and no entertainment but themselves.

Or it is ghosts, something in him suggested.

Thorbrand was afraid of neither man nor ghost, but he was properly respectful of the things he could not see. Well did he know that the hands that had built the cottage he stayed in were like as not bones beneath the earth he strode upon. For who abandoned a well-constructed cottage placed between two water sources? The pools to the back and the river below. Who walked off, leaving tools behind? No matter what theories were on offer in the nearest village.

The people who had lived here had either starved in a winter like this one, left for fear of that starving, or had died in one of the wars that always ravaged these lands. However they had left, some nights Thorbrand was certain he could see their handprints in the ash of the hearth. Reminding him that all men met their ends, like it or not, and not all ends were drenched in glory.

Perhaps not even his.

As he headed back across the still, cold valley today, he thought again about that island to the west. Black sand beaches and waterfalls cascading wherever he had looked. The wild sea like a wall of stone, rising again and again. But most of all, that land. New land.

Not soaked with blood and littered with bones. No ghosts, no ashy prints, no messes stretching back through time.

Land like this, Thorbrand could not help but think. A sturdy cottage, his woman, and at long last, quiet.

The quiet was his greatest indulgence. He was used to crowded halls and ships packed tight. Not a cottage to himself and his woman while outside, what looked like the whole world slumbered there before him without another living creature in sight. He knew not when he had last slept so deep, for he was not on his guard here, ready to leap into battle at a moment's notice. For no one was mounting a siege on this cottage. Only a few villagers in a different valley knew it stood here at all.

Thorbrand and Ulfric had stumbled upon it entirely by accident the previous winter when Ragnall had been making his move on Jorvik and the brothers had been forced, for reasons too tedious to recount, to make their own, far stealthier approach. Then, as now, there was naught in this valley but quiet days interrupted only by the wind and the odd bird.

Nor had he ever slaked his lust so long and so intensely, day after day, that he no longer felt certain that *lust* was the word to describe it. *Lust* was for some women, perhaps, but not Aelfwynn. Not his woman made of gold, who smiled at him when he was inside her and moaned out his name like one of her pretty Roman prayers.

Thorbrand had always intended to die in battle as his father had done. To carry on the family name, drenched in glory, a hero to his sons and their sons in turn. Making certain, blow by blow and battle after battle, that his failures did not pollute the family name. He had never understood a man who preferred plows to plunder.

But his time in this quiet valley had changed him.

Aelfwynn had changed him.

She was a prize. And she was his. And he found the conquering of her body, day and night, far sweeter a gift than any lands he might have taken in service to Ragnall. He knew it was true no matter how disloyal that might make him.

For he had come to know this valley, even covered in snow, in the same way he had learned Aelfwynn's curves and secrets. There was a poetry in walking the same land each day. In pitting his wits against what creatures lurked in so dark a season. The skalds might never sing these songs, but he could feel them in his heart. Changing him with their simple beauty.

He had always longed for the battlefields, but here, in the stillness that was only ever shattered by his woman's sweet cries, he found himself dreaming instead of the quiet verses a man could only hear when the land was not trod deep with the marching feet of too many armies.

But he knew too that he was a ruined man, doomed and grim. He was stained straight through with blood. He had watched his own parents die, had done naught to save them, and he had carried that curse through these brutal years. He carried it still.

The truth was, he did not deserve her.

Not her, not this quiet, and certainly not this peace.

It is as well, then, that this cannot last, he told himself gruffly.

For none of it would last. Not this. Not whatever life he built across the cold sea. That was his true duty, lest he forget. Nothing was his. He was Ragnall's.

He had always considered it a good bargain, before.

Thorbrand tried to shake his strange mood off as he made the final climb toward the cottage. Because however loath he might be to end this unexpected gift of time here, a surprise to himself each day, that did in no way alter Ragnall's plans for Aelfwynn.

Ragnall had made his wishes known, Thorbrand was sworn to uphold them, and that was the only story that would ever be told.

He would do the telling of it himself.

And there was no reason that should cut at him, the sharp edge of a knife he'd be far better off ignoring.

"I'm just as pleased you have no meat,"

Aelfwynn said brightly when he shouldered his way into the cottage, hands empty. The room was warm and smelled pleasingly of fresh bread. She had washed and hung some of their garments. And she was standing over her cauldron next to the fire, stirring something that smelled enticingly of fish and spice. "I have been in the dried fish and we will feast tonight."

But Thorbrand had a far different feast in mind.

He had taken her in a fury too many times to count. This afternoon, he shook off the snow and the cold, hanging what he could by the door. He watched her as he took off his boots, biting back a smile as she snuck glances at him while she applied herself to her stirring.

That he went over, held out his hand, and waited.

It was different, though he did not wish to ask himself why. It felt different, there in the places his chest squeezed tight when he gazed upon her. And he knew she felt it too when her golden eyes widened. She wiped her hands on the apron she'd made from what had once been her headdress. Then she put her hand in his.

Did he flatter himself that there was no longer anything but greed and longing in her gaze?

He led her to the pallet on the far wall and stood there with her for a moment, both her hands in his as he gazed down at her. He had tasted every part of her. He had learned her generous mouth with his own. He had brushed tears of pleasure from her cheeks. He knew her scent and her sounds.

You do not wish to share her with your king, a voice in him decreed, and he knew it for a truth. Little as he liked it.

For all that was his was Ragnall's. And Ragnall could do as he wished with it.

Even with Aelfwynn.

For the first time since he had been a lad of fifteen, battered and bruised, Thorbrand did not find that a comfort. He wanted her too much to know he must use her at another's command.

But then, he wanted everything too much. The quiet life, not merely a taste of it. All the things he knew he could never deserve. For too well did he know his worth—and it was the power in the swing of his sword. The vows he would not break. The trust his king had in him.

Sweet lives were for other men. Better men.

Men who were not drenched in blood, even when they were clean.

And well did Thorbrand know that the longer they tarried here, the sooner it was that Ragnall would call them to him and this would end. How was it possible he did not wish it to end? But he knew it was more than possible. He knew it, too, was a truth he would rather not face.

He who had faced all manner of unpleasant truths the way he did all things, with steel in his hand and the gods at his back.

"What troubles you, Thorbrand?" Aelfwynn whispered, those fire-bright eyes moving over his face.

"I need you," was all he could manage to say.

She sank down before him, his flaxenhaired princess, and settled herself prettily before him. Then, kneeling up, she put her hands on his thighs and waited for his nod. Thorbrand did not hesitate in giving it.

He pulled off his overtunic as she freed him from his trousers. She tugged them down his hips while he stripped off the linen tunic close to his skin. Then she leaned forward to lick him, delicately, around the thick head of his shaft.

First she teased him, running her tongue down his length, and pressing sweet kisses to the heavy pouch beneath. Then she repeated herself, light and maddening, until she found the head again, wrapped both hands around his length, and sucked him into her hot, wet mouth.

Thorbrand groaned and found her hair, sinking his fingers deep into the warm silk. He looked down the length of his body, for the sight never failed to stir him. Aelfwynn's blond hair flowing down her back, her face tipped up, and his thick length moving in and out of her pretty mouth.

He had taught her this and yet she still surprised him. She still shook him.

Soon she took him yet deeper, gripping his thighs when he took control. He thrust himself into her sweet, hot mouth again and again until he burst in a rush, roaring with pleasure as he emptied himself in her.

And then he felt the fire again, almost at once, when she sat back on her heels and smiled at him as she swallowed him down.

Everything was wild in him tonight. Thorbrand both did not know himself and knew himself too well. It was the only war he had to contend with of late. He could not swing his sword to cut down his dreams of quiet when he felt he should want glory for his family instead. And he could not vanquish glory when he had long since sworn that whatever glory might come to him, it would come in a lifetime's service to his king.

But Aelfwynn was here, not his king. And she was one of his vows.

He lifted Aelfwynn to her feet, then pulled off her overdress and her undershift. He bent to tug off her hose. Then he laid her out on his furs, a vision of breasts tipped in rose, golden eyes and pale gold hair, and the darker, richer gold between her thighs.

Thorbrand settled there, kneeling between her legs and drawing them over his shoulders as he set his mouth to her slick heat and drank his fill.

She yet tasted as he'd known she would, honey and heat, and all of it his. He knew how to make her arch up against him, how to grind her tender flesh against his mouth, his beard. He knew she liked the rough of his beard against her thighs, and the graze of his teeth while she bucked and sobbed.

And today he did not pull her astride him, or take her from behind. Or lie, side by side, where he could draw her leg over his hip.

Today, he crawled his way up the length of her body, licking her here, biting her gently there, and then, finally, gathered her beneath him. For the first time.

Aelfwynn's breath caught. Her eyes flew wide. "But…"

He had told her she need not lie upon her back to take him the first night he had worked the ache out of her limbs. And he had kept to that promise, but tonight… Tonight he wanted this.

Tonight he wanted her where he could see her, as if that might make the way she had bewitched him settle in him better.

"Do you trust me?" Thorbrand asked.

Slowly, even though she shook, Aelfwynn swallowed. Then nodded.

For the first time, Thorbrand stretched out on top of her and gazed down into her face. He gave her some of his weight and saw the way her eyes darkened with a deep, woman's pleasure. He gave her more and felt the tips of her breasts stiffen.

He took her hands in his and stretched her arms up high over her head, so that her breasts jutted up at the perfect level for him to take those stiffened peaks deep into his mouth.

And for a time, he only lay between her thighs, held her wrists in one hand, and helped himself to one breast, then the other. He kept on until she was writhing beneath him, making those high-pitched, greedy noises in the back of her throat that drove him wild.

But wild wasn't how he wanted her. Not tonight.

He put his free hand to one side of her head, held her gaze, and shifted his hips to thrust deep inside of her.

One thick, hard thrust, and he was seated within her.

His gaze was locked to hers. And so, caught there, he began to move.

Slowly.

He dragged himself out of her grip, then thrust in again. And he did not look away.

It was as if all the learning came to this. All the ways he made her scream. All that fire, all those storms. And here again was a quiet thing, yet no less a reckoning. Here was an intensity. An intimacy.

She wrecked him as surely as any battle.

Aelfwynn held him, her arms looped around his neck, and it became a rhythm between them, a sigh, a shift. And slowly, deliberately, they unraveled each other.

Then shattered into something new, together.

Later, she served him the stew she'd made and they ate on the floor before the fire, tangled up in each other as if they couldn't bear to let go. And that was where he took her again, stretched out so that the firelight danced all over the both of them, casting shadows and slicking them with heat. He rolled her beneath him, gathered her in his arms, and unraveled them again and again until all that was left was the two of them, wrapped up tight, his flesh still lodged in her, as if all that unraveling had woven them together after all.

Both of them wrecked, he thought. Both of them new.

And in the morning, the skies were clear. So too, the following day, was the sun so bright and the air so warm that the ice began to melt.

That night, he took her in a fury made new, something like desperate.

"Will you tell me what the matter is?" she asked softly, late in the night. She lay draped over him in his furs, her voice still ragged from the way she'd sat up to ride him, her hair falling between them. Like his very own Valkyrie.

"Nothing is the matter," he growled in return.

Then took her beneath him again to prove it.

And Thorbrand told himself he spoke truth, for come the morning, Leif and Ulfric were there to take them back to Ragnall.

Where he should have wanted to go, as he always had before.

Because it mattered not what Aelfwynn deserved, or what he knew he did not after all he'd done. It had never mattered. These days—and these dreams—were a distraction and no more.

Thorbrand had made vows, and he would keep them.

Chapter Ten

Widgongel wif word gespringeð; oft hy mon wommum biliho.

A far-wandering woman causes talk; often she is accused of sins.

—Maxims I, *The Exeter Book*

This, then, was the fate Aelfwynn had feared. Thorbrand's brother and cousin arrived with no warning. One moment it had been like any other morn in the cottage she had, foolishly perhaps, begun to consider *theirs*. She had been straining the mash she'd been using to make their ale, as she did every day before starting the bread for their dinner. Then the door had swung wide, letting the cold in. And Thorbrand was back again but with Leif and Ulfric with him, the three of them far too large for the cottage.

Oh, no, Aelfwynn thought at the sight of them. Distinctly. Because she very much doubted they were here for a family visit. Especially when Thorbrand's kin were clearly no less suspicious of her than the last time she'd seen them, weeks ago now.

They crowded into the cottage's single room, their sharp eyes missing nothing, she was certain. The laundry she'd hung yesterday. The pallet piled high with Thorbrand's furs. Her own head bared, her hair caught behind her in a long braid while she bent over her work, like some kind of slattern.

Aelfwynn hardly knew how to feel. She was sure she was as bright as the fire. Was it shame? Fear? Or was she upset at being disturbed here in this cottage, where she had come to think that being this man's thrall was…not quite the horror she'd anticipated?

Yet surely, she lectured herself sternly as the men talked loudly to each other in Irish, she had not imagined that she and Thorbrand could carry on like this forever. She could not possibly have thought any of this was truly hers.

Nor is he, she reminded herself sharply.

Not the way she had come to want him, she knew too well. A thrall had only what her master bought her and what he did with her was his own affair. That was the beginning and end of it.

No matter how her heart beat as if only for him.

Still, she did as required, no matter her feelings. She was no foolish girl who imagined *feelings* might sway men's minds. Especially not these men. Northmen, no less, who had laid in wait for her and carried her out of Mercia to serve their own ends. Aelfwynn quietly offered Ulfric and Leif hospitality and what food and drink she could. And fought to remain all that was serene when they condescended to speak with words she actually understood.

Though it was only to announce that they were leaving here to take her to their king.

"Our king commands your presence," Ulfric told her, a gleam in his dark eyes she could not say she cared for.

"And yours," Leif said to Thorbrand.

"I look forward to meeting such a legend,"

Aelfwynn said, as if easy with this turn of events.

What was far harder was when she looked at Thorbrand and saw no evidence of surprise on his face. She understood at once that he had expected this summons all along. That what had happened here had only ever been a bit of tarrying with his captive.

Did he suggest any other aim? a voice in her asked.

But Aelfwynn knew the answer already. The shame of it was hers. And so too the sin.

It took little time to pack up. Little time indeed to break apart the cottage she'd made more a home than it ought to have been until no trace of them remained. Aelfwynn knew from this that Thorbrand did not intend to return. What she could not know was how, somewhere in this quiet stretch of peaceful days threaded through with the wonders he worked with his body, she had let herself forget not only who she was—but who she was to him.

She blamed the way their bodies fit together. She blamed the heat of that spring and the surprising tenderness in the way Thorbrand fit his hand to her cheek. There was the temptation of his midnight gaze. The impossible beauty of his kiss. There were the scars that marked him, each and every one she had kissed while he'd told her a short, gruff story of how he'd survived the getting of it.

Trust well that the man who laid me open will never lift an axe again, he had growled once.

And that was the trouble, was it not? Aelfwynn had trusted him. Too well.

Maybe she wasn't as weak and foolish as she felt now, however, she thought as she drew her cloak around her and stepped out of the cottage to look out over the valley one last time. Maybe it had been the peace here, that was all. The simple joys of tending a fire and baking bread. Of making ale and washing their clothes. All the skills Mildrithe had insisted any charge of hers possess, and no matter who her parents were.

You are a woman first, child, she would say. *And there is no telling what sort of marriage you'll have.*

But it had been a long while since Aelfwynn had been given an opportunity to put her skills to the test. It was far different to help out than it was to take charge, and she found she liked it. Not that the work wasn't hard. It was. What work wasn't?

Yet she had found the simplicity of this life nothing less than a wonder. It had been what she'd hoped to find in Wilton Abbey. An order to her days and a reverence for that order, a far cry indeed from what her life had been like until now—both before and after her mother died.

More, she had found a deep joy in it because it was for him.

For Thorbrand.

She had let herself daydream…but there was nothing to be gained by dwelling on such things now. She pulled her hood tighter around her face while the men closed up the cottage and brought the horses round. There was a stiff, cold wind rushing down from the hills this morn and it felt too much like a slap in her face. But Aelfwynn welcomed it. Because the truth was, she should have known better. There was no safe, secluded space on this earth. Not for her.

Even if she had made it to the abbey as planned, had she truly believed that it would stand as a true sanctuary? Wherever people were, there were wars. It was only that they took a different shape in different places.

So too had this cottage been. They had fought in their own manner, had they not? Just because it felt good didn't make it any less of a battle, and Thorbrand had always been better at it. More skilled in every regard. Aelfwynn might have loved every moment, but that didn't make him any less the victor.

It made it sinful, that was all.

But she'd known that too. She'd known all of this. It was her fault for forgetting. Her fault for pretending this could be other than it was. Her own fault—and her shame.

When he hauled her up to ride before him once again, she had a thought that he might whisper something for her ear only. That he might tell her not to fear, or tell her what to expect. That he might offer her comfort.

Or hope, something in her added wistfully.

But he did not.

The three Northmen kicked their horses into a gallop and set off. And it had been what seemed like a lifetime since she'd last sat like this, before Thorbrand on the back of a horse. It felt familiar, yet also new. Because she knew his touch far better now. The press of his thigh against hers made her... melt. And this time, she did not try to pretend she felt it not.

Even though she rode to what must surely be her doom.

Again.

They rode for a few hours, this time keeping to the roads for a time, before veering off again and into the woods on a road less traveled. When they finally slowed, she expected to see a city worth the taking. But there was only a small village in another valley much like the one they'd stayed in.

"This cannot be York, can it?" she asked, confused.

"It would make little strategic sense to bring you into Jorvik," Thorbrand rumbled at her ear. "What if you were recognized?"

"Heaven forfend," she murmured, and took more pleasure in it than she should have when she could feel his laughter move his mighty chest behind her.

As if that might save her from what awaited her here.

Only then did it occur to her to worry about her reception here, so far north. She had no idea how Thorbrand's king treated his captives and slaves. All she'd ever heard about Ragnall was that he was a savage—but not one to underestimate. And even if she had not already listened well to her own mother rant about the Northmen who had fought these long years to reclaim Dublin and bring York under their rule, certainly she could not believe that Thorbrand would call any man king unless he was…an immensity.

But she dared not allow herself to think too much about it, lest she topple from the back of Thorbrand's horse in a dead faint, which would honor neither her nor her people.

She'd been sure that Thorbrand would do something to better indicate her status once they arrived amongst his own people. Bind her hands. Make her walk behind the horse in the trodden snow that had turned to mud. Cast her down before them, at the very least.

But instead, he rode her straight into the small village, sat up high on his steed for everyone to see.

Once again, Aelfwynn was forced to ask herself what it was Thorbrand wanted from her. What too his king might want. And unlike those first few days when they had ridden north with his kin, she thought she knew now. Was it possible Thorbrand had taken her to that cottage as…a test? She had heard whispers of such things in her uncle's court. Of women used and sold for pleasure, again and again. And not the woman's pleasure.

It would be a certain kind of man's idea of the perfect revenge.

Was Thorbrand that kind of man? Had she misjudged him so completely?

She cast down her eyes to block out the stares of the villagers who came out to watch as they rode in, and she could feel a surging, terrible panic inside her.

The truth was, her time in that cottage with Thorbrand had ruined her in more ways than one.

She felt as if she'd forgotten…everything. Who she was. What she was about. How to protect herself and how she might behave now that she found herself here. She knew already that whatever connection she might have imagined she felt with Thorbrand, it could not possibly matter.

Not here.

The three men stopped, and swung off the horses, though Thorbrand laid a heavy hand on Aelfwynn's leg and kept her where she was. High on his horse, visible to all who might gaze upon her.

He and his kin began to speak in Irish again, but she could hear other voices. The voices of the villagers here, speaking words she understood. And Aelfwynn could not decide if that was a gift or not. Perhaps it was a kindness not to comprehend what was happening to her.

Grace, she reminded herself. *This is an opportunity for grace.*

So she sat tall, though she was a Northman's slave. He could call her what he wished, she knew what blood she carried within her. She knew who she was.

No matter how he might have confused her with his touch, she knew.

Thorbrand turned from his brother and cousin and the other men who had come to join them in conversation. He came to the horse and lifted Aelfwynn off its back, an easy demonstration of his strength that should have terrified her. Instead, it made that flame inside her reach high.

He set her down, moving her to the front of him with his hand resting heavily on the nape of her neck.

Better that than an iron chain, she thought.

Aelfwynn tried her best to keep her gaze demurely lowered as he began to move, guiding her before him so she might walk when he did. She expected jeers, perhaps. Shouts. Even the odd stone, but all was silent. Eerily so.

Soon enough they reached the longhouse that stood at the center of the village with smaller cottages and the other buildings necessary to village life arrayed around it. Though unlike other villages, where the people came and went freely from the communal places, men stood at the off-center door and eyed her coldly.

Aelfwynn tried her best to look serenely unconcerned, though she feared her hands shook.

Then the men opened the door, Thorbrand thrust her forward, and she found herself in the presence of the Northman king who would have killed her mother, if he could. Ragnall, whose name had only ever been spoken in her presence in these last years as a curse.

There were others in the hall, dark and smoky, but she knew him instantly. It was how he sat at the great chair at the far end with an appearance of languor that was utterly belied by the power in his gaze and the authority that sat on him like armor.

This was Ragnall, the scourge of Dublin even before the Irish kings had expelled him and other Northmen who had originally come from Norway, yet had long since mixed with the natives. Ragnall who had taken the Isles and had moved on to Northumbria. Rumored to be a direct descendant of Ivar the Boneless, though there were many who claimed such things around a fire on a cold night. Rumored too to be a man of dark appetites and darker grudges, Ragnall wreaked havoc wherever he went, and the way he looked at her suggested he would think it a pleasure indeed to turn his dark attentions on her. She reminded herself that true though all those stories and rumors might be, he was yet a man.

Just a man, flesh and blood like any other.

But that had never comforted her when it was her uncle who stood before her, her life in his hands. Nor did it aid her overmuch now as Thorbrand marched her down the center of the hall to stop before his king's chair.

Ragnall was not a young man, though he yet had power written deep all over him.

There was gray on his head and in his beard, but his gaze pierced straight through her.

"Aethelflaed's daughter," the king said, after all those around him had stopped speaking in Irish. In a tone of great satisfaction. "You have the look of her."

It was as if Aelfwynn had been in a dream. There had been nothing but snow, the wind howling around the cottage so intensely she'd been certain they would wake to find no roof above them. And she would not have cared, for the wonder that she experienced again and again at Thorbrand's hands.

Not only his hands. His mouth. Every part of his marvelous body. And that impossible magic when he thrust deep inside her.

What she could not understand was how, when such sensations existed, she had lived her whole life having no idea they were possible. She had found herself staring off into space when she should have been mending, or tending to the fire and her many other tasks, asking herself who of the people she knew could possibly have experienced these things. How could it be that they had walked next to her in this state and she had never known it?

For even if she now understood a need so

great that any dark corner would do, she found it difficult to believe that people simply lived their lives, breathing the same air she did, when they had ever felt... Like this. Like new.

And she had lost herself in it so completely that even the arrival of his disapproving kin hadn't brought her back to herself. Even traveling through this village, for all she had braced herself, hadn't quite done it. For there was Thorbrand's heavy hand at her neck and the traitorous slickness between her legs.

But here, now, was her mother's name in an enemy's mouth.

And Aelfwynn might have felt a pang about letting go of all that rich, wondrous heat that had so marked these past weeks. But let it go she did.

Because she was, indeed, her mother's daughter.

She inclined her head. "You have the advantage, I think. You invoke my mother's name, yet I do not recall her ever having uttered yours in my hearing."

And then she smiled.

Thorbrand's hand tightened at her nape. The men who stood around Ragnall's chair stiffened in outrage.

But Ragnall laughed.

He threw back his head and roared loud enough that all the others in the room shifted their battle-ready stances and joined in. Though behind her, she could feel no less tension in the way Thorbrand continued to grip the nape of her neck. Or the way he stood close, the wall of his chest at her back. Almost as if he meant to protect her—

She knew that could never be so.

"Are you certain?" Ragnall asked when he finished laughing, and though there was mirth on his craggy face, she did not mistake the shrewdness in the way he gazed at her. "Perhaps she cried it last, upon her deathbed. Knowing then, as she should have known before, that Jorvik was already mine."

"I fear not," Aelfwynn murmured. "It is said she asked only for a sword to handle the fight herself. If she had, who knows who would claim Jorvik today?"

Ragnall laughed again, louder this time, and Aelfwynn knew her gambit had succeeded.

You must learn how to recognize and measure a man, her mother had always said. *It is how they carry themselves. How pride*

works in them, and envy. Some men are
bold because they believe they have noth-
ing to prove. Prefer these men, always, to
those who have everything to prove and
will use any opportunity to show it to be so.
They love nothing better than crushing those
weaker than themselves. Never give them the
opportunity.

Handy as that advice might have been,
Aelfwynn did not forget herself. She was
not her mother, the mighty Lady of the Mercians, who would have spoken to Ragnall as
if they were the same. Whether he considered himself such or did not, Aethelflaed had
still been who she was. A woman of standing,
with armies at her beck and call. Aelfwynn,
by contrast, was slave to one of his men. A
thrall who any one of them could use as they
wished if Thorbrand allowed it—and she had
no doubt that some of the greedy, considering gazes she felt upon her came from men
who could think of any number of ways they
might like to test a woman who dared speak
to their leader so.

She cast her eyes down once again, kept her
pretty smile on her face, and did her best to
look nothing at all but peaceful. Even when

they continued to discuss her, as if she was not there, in the language they must have all known by now she could not understand. It was clearly meant to put her in her place after all.

And Aelfwynn counted herself lucky enough it wasn't a blow.

The voices got louder, then dropped. When she dared sneak a glance, she found Ragnall was staring at her again, no hint of good humor on his face.

She found she did not have to *try* to act meekly any longer.

"Tell me of your uncle." And though Ragnall's voice was an invitation, she was perfectly aware that it was a command.

Again, Thorbrand's grip at her neck tightened. And Aelfwynn had the strangest notion that he was not issuing his own commands, he was attempting to…comfort her. Or speak with her, somehow, without anyone else the wiser.

That is naught but a wish, she told herself sternly. But somehow, wish or no, it made the tension inside her settle all the same.

"My uncle is well," she replied to the Northman king. "Hale and hearty when I saw him last, in truth."

"And does he move on Jorvik?" Ragnall asked in reply, his voice significantly less inviting than before. His smile a blade. "Or does he content himself with weaseling his way into Nottingham, thinking, as your mother did, that building your fortresses will keep us out?"

What Aelfwynn knew was what she felt certain every man in this hall knew. That Nottingham had strategic value thanks to its position on the Trent. And that her uncle had repaired its defenses and then manned it with his own people and Danes alike, the better to appease the many Danes who were as displeased with the Northman incursion as he was. Such as those who had conspired with her mother against Ragnall last year.

But no good could come of her saying such things.

"I know not," Aelfwynn managed to say, keeping her gaze on Ragnall. "My uncle did not see fit to confide his plans in me. And indeed, if your man is correct, sought to kill me off altogether."

"Your family is not as close as mine, I

take it," Ragnall said, and though his eyes gleamed, it was all those around him who laughed.

"It's these Saxons," Leif boomed out. "More concerned with building their walls than taking care of their own families."

"You mistake the matter." Aelfwynn felt her chin rise, and though she knew she risked herself—and Thorbrand's grip on her neck let her know how much—she could not stop herself. "My uncle and his sister were close, but the same cannot be said for him and me. They knew each other well and had done so since they were young. In comparison, my motivations can only be guessed at."

The Northman king sat forward, his gaze so hard it made her want to shrivel. Yet she did not. And deep inside, she accepted that it was because Thorbrand was there, holding her up.

"What, then, are your motivations?" Ragnall demanded, no laughter anywhere about him. "And do not dissemble. I cannot abide a lie in the mouth of a woman."

"No man who lies to his king is a man at all," Ulfric intoned darkly.

"My motivation at present," Aelfwynn said crisply, "is to escape my captor and flee. I think you'll find it is the primary motivation of any captive."

Yet because she smiled when she said it, Ragnall laughed again.

"Ragnall is not her king," Thorbrand added then, his voice dark. Darker than usual, commanding the instant attention of all in the hall, including Ragnall. And reminding Aelfwynn that he, too, had weapons greater than steel. "Edward is her king as well as her uncle. We forget it at our peril, surely."

"It would be treasonous to say otherwise," Aelfwynn agreed, still smiling. "No matter how many men lay in wait for me on that road."

Ragnall considered her. "But it is not up to a woman loyal to the Wessex king to decide where her loyalty lies. A Christian woman must have a master, is that not so?"

"I am blessed with many," Aelfwynn replied, though she shook, deep inside. "Beginning with my God, master of all masters."

"They say you are a pious thing above all else," the Northman king continued, thoughtfully. He stroked his beard as he gazed down at Aelfwynn. "It is said that no matter who was chosen for you by your mother, you would have given your agreement, and so she could use you in any manner she saw fit."

"I was never given the opportunity to prove my obedience," Aelfwynn replied, carefully, and was glad of it that she could not see Thorbrand, then. For she had obeyed him, had she not? Over and over and over again.

"You must know that I could have you killed at any time," Ragnall said, almost softly. Almost. "It is a tidy solution, as your uncle knew well. For as long as you draw breath, you remind too many that your mother held Mercia and a man who marries you could do the same. With or without your uncle's approval. I considered having my men cut your throat and deliver you thus to your uncle. A message I know well he would understand. For however he might choose to treat his own blood, he would not take kindly to my doing the same."

Aelfwynn inclined her head, and tried to look suitably grateful for his counsel. Even if what he had to say was this. And even when her throat began to ache in protest of his talk of cutting it.

"But I would have died long since were I blind to the tools presented to me," Ragnall growled at her. "No matter their form. And as long as you are useful, girl, I will keep you alive."

He stared at her, and Aelfwynn had to fight off the icy cold trickle that wound its way down the length of her back. He stared at her from his high seat and she knew that once again, she was helpless. Was that not always her plight?

Her mother would have fought—

Your mother is dead, a voice in her said sharply. *You can choose to follow her, or you can choose to live. But you must choose. Now.*

And so Aelfwynn discovered that she was not, in fact, a martyr. Because she wished to live. There was Thorbrand at her back, no matter what these men had in store for her, and she wished to *live*.

"Then I vow it is my great delight to prove myself useful to you," she told the Northman king. And bowed her head.

Her mother would have been appalled. But Aethelflaed was not here. And Aelfwynn was in no rush to follow her into the hereafter.

There was a small, tense silence, and she was certain that meant they were all speaking to each other with their eyes over her head.

Let them, she thought. The outcome would be the same—as they wished it—whether she joined in or did not.

"Until tomorrow, then," Ragnall said, after the silence had gone on some little while.

Though her lashes were low, she was aware of it when he swaggered from the hall, his men with him. Even Leif and Ulfric left, and slowly, almost as if he didn't want to do it, Thorbrand turned her around so she was looking straight at him.

She reacquainted herself with his face. It had been a long while since she had gone so long without seeing it. Midnight eyes and a dark beard of the same rich, deep brown as his hair, the sides braided back. He was a fearsome sight, this man. He was beautiful.

But he had never been hers.

Aelfwynn needed to take that to heart and quick.

Thorbrand ran his hand over her long plait. "Not many dare to taunt my king."

"The best kings like to be taunted," Aelfwynn replied. "In moderation. For them, it is a moment's amusement to be treated as if they are ordinary."

"Is that what you are, Aelfwynn? A moment's amusement?"

"Is that up to me?" She searched his face but saw only stone. "I thought it was required of me that I make myself a useful tool."

Thorbrand's gaze was a torment, then. He had dropped the hand that had tugged on her braid, but his other hand still caught her nape. And as he gazed down at her, his thumb moved. Up, then down, spreading heat deep into her.

Reminding her that where he was concerned, all she ever did was burn.

His thumb stopped moving. "Then I will tell you what it is Ragnall requires of you."

There was a heaviness in his tone and she could have sworn she saw some kind of bleakness in his gaze. But his eyes stayed steady on hers, even so.

She remembered their first time in the hot spring and the taut, intense look on his face as he'd held her splayed open. *You are the daughter of kings and queens,* he had told her. *And you will suffer beautifully. And quietly.*

Aelfwynn gathered those words to her breast. She stood straight. Then held his gaze, as if she had no fear.

"Ragnall wishes for your loyalty," Thorbrand told her. "To him alone."

Aelfwynn was sure she did not react, but when Thorbrand smiled, she knew she had failed.

"As he was at pains to discover himself, I already have a king," she said slowly. Carefully. Very carefully. "For all his faults, Edward must claim my loyalty. Even if for blood alone."

"That is why he spoke to you of masters." Thorbrand's gaze was hot, then. Another weapon, she thought distantly. "For the day will come when Ragnall takes Mercia, Aelfwynn. And it will be easier to settle, will it not, if your people see that they are not being conquered by savages, but rather reintroduced to one they already know well and love."

Aelfwynn swallowed hard and willed her hands not to curl into fists.

"I think you underestimate the Mercian spirit, Thorbrand." She forced herself to breathe. To broach the topic she had avoided all this time, because, she understood, she had been too afraid to face it. But face it she must. "For they will not celebrate the daughter of their much-beloved Lady when she arrives before them in chains. As a thrall to a conqueror."

He laughed. He *laughed*, and she hated him with a wild passion in that moment, but it did naught to stop him. "You think I will make you my thrall? In chains?"

And she had known, always, that this day would come, had she not? It had been particularly clear on the cold ride here what was likely to happen to her. What would become of her. All she had left was her dignity.

If all else failed, she would rely on it. It would not save her. She knew that.

But it was far better than shame.

"I have accepted my fate," she told him, proud of how clear her voice was. "I would have thought that you would cheer on my acquiescence. Is that not how you Northmen embrace your destiny?"

Thorbrand studied her, his laughter fading. There, alone in the hall, he moved to slide his hands to her face. Then he held her there, a palm on either side and a look she was sure she had never seen before making him look... new.

She would have said *tender* had his eyes not blazed.

"I am sorry indeed to disappoint you," he said in that dark, stirring way that she feared would always make her bones go soft. And the rest of her burn. "But I have not taken you to become my thrall. I have no need of you as a slave."

She did not understand. What was worse than a thrall? Her mouth was far too dry of a sudden. "Then…?"

"Aelfwynn, I thought you knew." Thorbrand did not smile. His mouth was stern, his gaze intense. And she could feel that crackling fire that was always between them leap high. "I will have you for my wife. On the morrow."

Chapter Eleven

~~~~~~~~~

Man må hyle med de ulve man er i blandt.

One must howl with the wolves one is
among.

—Old Norse Proverb

The next morning, Thorbrand left Aelfwynn
sleeping soundly in his furs, tucked up in the
tent he'd pitched behind the long hall before
the main meal the night before. Where, later
that same eve, he had indulged every impulse
he'd put on hold during their first nights in
that same tent. And had acquainted her with
almost every one of the images he'd kept to
himself back in those early days—saving only
those that required...more space. And fewer
nearby ears.

He stretched as he stood outside the tent,

pleased to see another bright winter's day with
no hint of any more snow in the air. The villagers were tending to the cattle and the sheep
this side of the morning meal, though he could
see the smoke rise above the hall and the rich
scent of last night's stew that would feed the
adults a bit later. His belly let him know it was
empty, but he liked to have little food in him
when he trained.

Instead of making his way into the hall, he
skirted the building to meet up with Ulfric,
Leif, and the rest of the men who had come
with Ragnall. They gathered out in the fields
to swing steel and make certain that whatever
came next, they were ready.

As he had always been ready, Thorbrand
thought as he and Leif battled, warming
quickly enough in the cold that soon, they
steamed. Their swords clashed and neither one
of them was afraid to fight dirty. Leif laughed
loud and long as he fought, a tactic Thorbrand
had seen unnerve a great many opponents in
their time, but he knew his cousin well. He
ignored the bluster and aimed for the other
man's weaknesses.

And smiled when his cousin stopped laughing and cursed him instead.

"You rely too much on the noise you make," Thorbrand told him.

"Meyla krafla mikli thur syr," Leif growled back.

Thorbrand only grinned at the colorful insult. "That is no way to speak of your aunt, cousin."

Leif lifted his sword and charged.

And all around them, men grunted and fought, holding themselves in check only enough to keep from skewering their brothers. Steel clashed and sang. Men cursed and boasted. These were the sounds that brought the world awake each morn and lulled it to sleep each night, and well did Thorbrand know it.

The gods forged the earth, but men bled upon it. Son after father, season after season. His own sons would chase their honor and glory on these cold islands, until all that was left of his blood was a whisper on the wind and, if he was lucky, a story told well over a warm fire on a cold night.

It was the gift his own deeds gave his father before him.

There was a time such thoughts had brought him comfort.

But as the morning passed in the clang of steel and the roar of battle, even though it were practice, he found the notion less pleasant than before.

Imagine, a voice inside him whispered, to his shame, *if you honored your parents not by dying as they did...but by living?*

He could not imagine such a shameful life, he told himself as he fought.

Yet he knew that the real trouble was that he could.

Thanks to Aelfwynn and their time in that cottage, he could indeed.

When they had finished, the men made their way into the hall, where the village women had warmed last night's stew and ladled it out to all as they took seats where they could. This was a farming village, not a warrior's mead hall, and there were no storied long tables here. It was how his people lived through the winters and the wars, Thorbrand thought as he took his meal and sat. The raiders sailed with provisions enough to live through a long siege in a hostile place. They dried out fish so it could be easily carried and stored, then left in water so it could be eaten as new wherever they found themselves should the journey be overlong or hunting prospects meager where they landed. And they could sleep in their sturdy tents no matter the weather, as Thorbrand had done all over these islands, more often than not. But what a man *could* do was not necessarily what he liked to do. He far preferred a welcome like this instead, with a rich stew to warm his belly and the heat of a well-tended fire when the weather turned. Though this village was more in the Saxon style than that of Thorbrand's people, the villagers here no doubt a mix of Northumbrian and the many invaders who had claimed these lands, they had greeted Ragnall as their king.

Because survival often depended on recognizing a king when one appeared, Thorbrand thought then, with some amusement. He suspected that were Edward to appear before this same hearth tomorrow, the villagers would treat him just the same.

Kings came and went. Land could always be disputed. What mattered was the will to fight on, come what may.

Then again, he thought as he filled his belly, perhaps there were other ways to fight.

"How fares our Mercian princess with her

upcoming nuptials?" Ulfric asked from beside him. "She will make a merry bride, I hope?"

Thorbrand shrugged. "I feel certain she will come around to it."

Leif snorted. "However will you tempt her?"

"I do not find it necessary to tempt women, cousin," Thorbrand said. He grinned. "They find merely to gaze upon me temptation enough."

"Temptation enough to slip a dagger in your ribs," his brother retorted.

"And yet I do not bleed," Thorbrand replied. He eyed Ulfric and his usual dark scowl. "A pity you cannot say the same, brother."

Ulfric glared, the scar on his face telling its own tale. And then Leif was starting in on him as Thorbrand had known he would, once again bringing up the fact that Ulfric, a mighty warrior, had let his own concubine cut him.

Thorbrand sat back, let them bicker, and thought over Aelfwynn's reaction to the news he meant to wed her.

It had been much like that first night in their tent, after he'd taken her from the road. That night she had laid herself out before him, a brave sacrifice to a ravening beast.

And had seemed, if he wasn't mistaken, somewhat disappointed that her martyrdom was not required.

So too had she seemed…almost outraged that he planned to marry her.

You do not mean marry *me,* she'd said, her voice loud and shocked in the empty hall.

And yet I will, all the same.

She had frowned at him, that perfect, placid sweetness of hers gone as if it had never been. That mask she wore to handle kings and strangers alike had disappeared like smoke through the opening in the roof above them.

He found he liked it best when she wore no mask at all. And no garments otherwise, were he to have his way.

I'm not the loose end your king believes me to be, she had told him. *My uncle wanted me dead. Or at the very least, tucked away in a nunnery with unbreakable vows made to God. I am no threat to anyone.*

Thorbrand had considered her for some time. And wondered what had befallen him, that while he yearned to ease his need in her, as ever, he found a different solace simply in touching her. In holding her face in his hands.

In running hands over the silk of her flaxen tresses, braided or not.

It is not that you are a threat, sweeting, he told her, and had found a hand over his chest as if he was bruised. *It is that you could be used as leverage. Surely you know this.*

Her frown had deepened. *I do not recall agreeing to marry anyone, much less the man who abducted me from a dark road.*

You cannot have imagined the choice would ever have been yours to make, Aelfwynn. Whether on a dark road or in a bright-lit castle.

She had actually curled her hands into fists. He would have laughed, if only to see if she would swing them, but this was a serious matter. This was their marriage—and he found that what he'd seen as a duty to be exercised in service to his king before he'd met her was now…

A different kind of song in him altogether.

I do not know how you Northmen conduct your affairs, she had seethed at him, *but brides are rarely forced where I come from. We are not so uncivilized as some.*

He had wanted to stop her there. To revel in her like this, eyes of molten gold no longer demurely downcast. Temper coloring her cheeks. Those *fists*. Like his very own, tiny Saxon Valkyrie. His cock took notice. His heart had pounded at him, hard, like a blow.

But Ragnall expected a wedding to lock Aelfwynn down and keep her within his control, to be used against her uncle in the future. And it turned out… Thorbrand wanted a wedding himself, for reasons he had not cared to dig into just then.

This is no question of civility, he had told her. *It is about kingdoms, not manners. You are the granddaughter of Alfred. It is known what blood runs in your veins.*

Remember who my mother was, please.

I remember, he had said. *Though I wonder if you do. She loved you well, I have no doubt, but surely you know that when it came to a choice between her love and her rule, she would always have chosen what was best for Mercia. Or perhaps for her brother.*

She would never have forced me, Aelfwynn had protested.

I assume she would have but asked you.

Aelfwynn had clearly misliked his dry tone. *If I had found a man disgusting, she would never have insisted I wed him.*

Happily, that is not our situation, he had said, perhaps more darkly than before. For he had begun to find that her resistance to the idea of wedding him did not sit well with him. *Well do I think you know it.*

What is it you plan to do? she had asked, holding herself still. Too still. *You marry me at your king's behest, but then what? March on Mercia before the week ends?*

Thorbrand had studied her for a moment while he made sure his own temper stayed in check. *Ragnall must fortify his position as King of Jorvik. Only once he has done so, and thrown open trading routes with our kin in Dublin, will we advance. And you will be a part of that, as my wife.*

He had not chosen to point out that he would never have discussed such things with her had he not known, without doubt, that she would wed him. It was to his own detriment that he wanted also for her to *wish* to do so.

Though he had thought he would rather die than admit such a thing.

I will never be a part of any plot that threatens Mercia, she had gritted at him. *Never.*

Then tell yourself, here and now, that you will make yourself easy with what must come, he had told her, his voice like steel. *For this is the way of the world, Aelfwynn. And you know it. Mercia will fall. Whether it is to Ragnall, to your uncle, or to whoever rises up when all of us are dead. Should Ragnall prevail it will be my honor to rule Mercia in concert with his wishes and with Aethelflaed's daughter at my side. And you may lie to yourself if it pleases you, but both of us know well that taking your place at the side of a man who might otherwise be an enemy has always been your purpose.*

But...

Thorbrand had not finished. *And well too do you know that marrying me will not be the sacrifice you might have been called upon to make, were the choice your mother's.*

She had turned her head away at that, but he'd seen the heat in her gaze and the glassiness as much from that as from the force of her emotions. He had taken her chin and pulled her face back to his.

We have already lived as a man and wife do, he had gritted at her. *You may well be carrying my child. And I do not intend for my sons to be illegitimate.*

And not only because he did not think Edward of Wessex would pay for the raising of a son he did not claim, or a part of the raising if Thorbrand acknowledged him, as was his people's custom.

That's a very convincing offer, she had begun, her golden eyes shooting sparks at him as though they stood in a forge.

That is no offer, sweeting. Those are simple truths. The offer is this. He had searched her face, his grip gentle enough but his own gaze a fury. *Us.*

And what use will such a thing as us *be when you are off dying on a battlefield?* she had hissed at him. *Chasing your glory while the women you leave behind must grieve your death and plan your burial.*

This is what men must do.

This is what men do, yes, she had replied hotly. *But whether they* must *is a different matter. I will be a widow within a year, and then what? Will your king hand me off to your brother? Your cousin? Not that it will matter to you, dead and gone.*

Thorbrand had not liked any of that. It had struck him then that he had never thought of his mother's pain. Only her courage. But he should have known better. Courage was not called for where there was naught but joy. And was that the life he wanted for his woman made of gold? Ever waiting, ever worrying. Raising his sons to mourn him.

Sending them off to die in his footsteps.

Did he dare imagine there was anything else for a man as battle-scarred as he was?

Or was that little more than a betrayal of those he should have saved?

Neither you nor I will be dying near any battlefield, Aelfwynn. I cannot risk another happening along and finding you, then using you as we would. And he had not wished to ask himself if it was Ragnall he thought of then. Or if it was only himself. *I want you to be my weapon, not anyone else's. There is a new land in the west. A new island. I have been there, and I will take you back, and we will live there as we already have.* It had taken him a moment to recollect himself. *Until it is time.*

You, Thorbrand? she had asked softly, though he had heard too well the disquiet in her voice. *You intend to live quietly, far away from blood and glory? I don't believe it.*

Neither did he. But it ached in him, the wanting of it.

And then the villagers had come in to claim their hall that had likely only just been emptied of the animals that slumbered within during the cold season, and he had not seen her again, alone, until it was time for them to take to their tent. For Aelfwynn had busied herself with the work of the women, tending to the stores brought out to acknowledge Ragnall's presence and the meat the king had brought as tribute to his hosts' generosity. There had been drinking aplenty and bright songs sung.

Inside their tent last night, it had been dark. Close. He'd had her on her hands and knees, gripping that flaxen hair that fell all around her and pulling her head back as he slammed himself into her, telling her without words how this would always be with them.

And he had taken her mouth while he'd done it, for she was far sweeter a taste on his tongue than the mead he'd drunk.

He'd woken in the night to find her wrapped all around him as was her custom, her leg drawn over his. He had rolled over, drawing her legs wide so he could slide inside, knowing she loved to shiver awake to find him already deep within her.

He had not spoken then, either.

And it was only now, with his brother and cousin trading barbs and his king's men all around him, that it occurred to him she had not answered him. She had managed, somehow, not to tell him whether she would marry him, however reluctantly, or if she planned to cause difficulties.

Thorbrand had assumed her body's soft surrender was her answer...but Aelfwynn was unlike other women he had known. He wanted her words. He wanted a vow.

He wanted something that was his alone.

Even if only for a small while, away across the sea, before the world swallowed them down again.

She was not in the hall. He went out to look for her throughout the village, but couldn't find her in the groups of women he found tending to the usual tasks of the day. He searched the whole of the village, twice, before he found himself standing at the fencing that kept the animals in and the beasts out. Or tried.

"I have not seen your woman this morn," came the voice of his king from behind him.

Thorbrand turned and nodded his greeting. "It could be she hides," he said, though that was unlike the woman he thought he knew. "She had resigned herself to slavery, you understand. That she has been elevated to a bride offends her."

Ragnall laughed. He was yet a mighty force of a man, though he was far more gray in person than he ever was in Thorbrand's memories. Yet only a fool with a death wish would discount the damage he could still do well with his blade. He held himself like the king he was, but to Thorbrand, he had always been more than that.

He was the father who had lived.

And more, the father who had never looked at him and found him wanting.

"You do me a great service, Thorbrand," Ragnall said after a moment, his gaze on the fields. "There remains no one else I could trust with such a task, as I have told you."

"It is my honor," Thorbrand said gruffly. "You know this is so."

"What I know is that you think the only honor to be found in this brutal life is in battle. And well have you distinguished yourself there. Many a song will be sung of you, but none, I think, as rich as this task you undertake."

"A man kidnaps a woman and removes himself to a distant land, where he seeks out a distant cousin, become a chieftain, and farms," Thorbrand said dryly. "This is not the great story of our age, I suspect."

"But you must keep her safe, no matter who comes," Ragnall countered. "Never must her name be spoken again in halls where men listen, lest our enemies seek her out and use her for their own ends. You may till a field if you wish, but it can only come second to your real duty. And more, I know you will do it. You will not throw her overboard and tell me it was an accident, so you might return to the battles that might win you the glory others seek. You will not abuse her. You will keep her, for me, until I have need of her here."

Thorbrand nodded, for what else could he do? He would do what Ragnall asked, because he asked. Because *he* asked, whether he was king or no, and Thorbrand owed him his life. His years at Ragnall's side had let him, if not make up for what he had done, find an ease in it. And because this was so, whatever Ragnall wished to make of his life would be done. Thorbrand would see it done.

They stood there together, looking out at

the cold afternoon. The sky was clear and what light there was, on the brighter side of midwinter, cast the land around them into hue less bleak than usual.

And Thorbrand knew he must offer his king what everything in him roared against.

Even if it tested the loyalty he would have sworn, before, was as solid as any mountain.

"You could take her for yourself," he made himself say, though it felt ripped from the deepest part of him. "Instead of spinning out these plots."

Ragnall sent him a sideways glance, filled with laughter. "Could I, then? And you would surrender her, would you?"

"You are my king," Thorbrand gritted out.

Ragnall laughed out loud and clapped him on the shoulder. "This is why I chose you, Thorbrand. Your loyalty extends so far you would hand over your woman, who could even now grow thick with your child. But I do not require this of you."

Thorbrand had made the offer because he felt he must. Because Ragnall should have first choice, even when it came to Aelfwynn. Though the words had tasted rotten on his tongue, he had forced himself to speak them anyway.

But now that Ragnall had refused, something in him…shuddered.

Relief, he knew.

Because he was not as loyal as his king believed him. For even as he'd spoken the hateful words, he had known the truth.

He would not let Aelfwynn go without a fight. Even if it were necessary he fight his own king.

The man he considered a father.

"It would be impossible to hide her until the right moment if she was with me," Ragnall was saying. "Her whereabouts would be known, her people notified. It would give Edward an excuse to rise against me before I wish it. And besides, I have all the concubines I can handle. I do not need one who considers herself a princess."

He laughed at that, and Thorbrand smiled too, for he knew some of his king's concubines too well. He had separated them from each other in more than one brawl.

"They fight enough as it is," he said.

"I have always admired those who long for a quiet life," Ragnall told him. "But the gods set me on a different path. Not for me the plow. Instead I will swing a steel blade until the fight claims me, and hope I make my way to Valhalla. We all must play our part. Lucky is the man who can play more than one."

"And what would you do," Thorbrand asked him, "if there were no end? If you swept the whole of this island and called it your own. If the world fell before you. Where would you fight then?"

His king studied him a moment. "Northmen will take these islands. If not in my time, then those who come after me will make it so. I believe this."

Thorbrand nodded.

"And there is always a fight, Thorbrand," Ragnall continued, with a grin. "Always, everywhere, there are kings with too much land. All I seek is to part them from it. I am a simple man."

Thorbrand couldn't stop thinking about that as he continued looking for Aelfwynn.

For he had discovered that he, too, was a simple man. He wanted land like any other. Riches enough to hold what was his and more friends than enemies.

But most of all, he wanted Aelfwynn.

For it had never occurred to him that she might not wish to marry him.

He did not like that at all. Thus it took him far too long to realize, when he still couldn't find her, that she had given him her answer after all.

And run.

Chapter Twelve

〰〰〰

*Leorna a hwæthwugu; ðeah ðe þine gesælða
forlætan, ne forlætt þe no þin cræft.*

Always be learning something; though
your good fortune may abandon you, don't
abandon your skill.

—Old English *Dicts of Cato*,
translated by Eleanor Parker

Aelfwynn only vaguely recognized the
wiry Northman who waited there when she
emerged from her tent that morning. She
had woken to find Thorbrand gone, but as
she'd lain there surrounded by his scent in the
warmth of his furs, there had been no mys-
tery as to where he'd gone. She could hear the
shouts of the men. The clash of swords in the
distance that reminded her where she was.

Not in the secluded cottage she'd come to consider a home. Nor even back out in the cold woods of Mercia and the Danelaw as she'd been those first few days with Thorbrand and his disapproving kin. She was in a tiny village in southern Northumbria, likely no great distance from York. And yet far enough that Ragnall was not over worried about the villagers recognizing Aelfwynn, or her name, and carrying the tale of the Lady of the Mercians' daughter in the Northman clutches to others.

All this had she discerned the night before, while she'd quietly helped the village women prepare and serve all the men, the village's own hardy male folk and the warriors who had come with the king.

An honor, is it? muttered one of the women, old and round with years and clearly in charge of what went on around the hearth in the village's central hall. *We are fair lousy with kings, we are.*

All the women had fallen silent, sneaking looks at Aelfwynn out of the corner of their eyes at words that could have been considered treasonous when there was only one king about at present.

Kings are only men, are they not? Aelfwynn had asked mildly as she'd stirred the stew in the great pot. She had looked at no one, as if she hadn't noticed the possible harm in the older woman's words. *And what man does not wish to imagine he is the only one?*

The other women had laughed loud at that, their manner notably warming. Leaving Aelfwynn to wonder how she'd done without this for all her years. For there had always been a separation between her and the rest of the women. How could there not be, no matter the grace in her manner or her willingness to help? She was like them, yet not. She helped as she could, as all women must, but all had been far too aware that she was only ever a moment away from being called to her mother's side. Or in the last six-month or so, too busy fending off all her would-be advisors and swains.

But here she was naught but another pair of hands.

It was in that spirit, still full to bursting with all that happy anonymity she had never before tasted, that she smiled politely enough at the man who waited for her outside the tent.

"Come," he ordered her, severely.

Aelfwynn placed him as one of Ragnall's

men. He had been there when Thorbrand had first brought her before his king. He had stood to one side of Ragnall's great chair and the way he had looked at her had in no way been friendly. But this hardly distinguished him from the rest. She had dismissed him—as all of them—as yet one more Northman, and certainly not the one she most feared.

Because there was only one Northman she truly feared, and for all his authority and might, it was not Ragnall. It was the one who claimed he would marry her. Today.

And it was as if, after spending a lifetime learning how to choose decorum above all else, Aelfwynn had completely forgot how on earth she had ever done such things. How she could possibly keep her feelings contained when it seemed far more likely they would eat her whole, like a fearsome monster from one of the old tales the skalds told on cold winter nights in her mother's halls.

It would have been easier to fight a monster. Aelfwynn knew not how she could fight *herself.*

She followed the man willingly enough. He led her away from the sounds of men's cries and the clash and clamor of their swords, the rough music that made the world into elegies sung around mournful hearths and ever would. They walked back to the far boundary of the village, then set off across a frigid field toward the ever-waiting wood.

The trees stood like ghosts, cold branches bare and braced against the morning sky with its low light in the distance.

"Where do you take me?" she asked of her silent companion, who stalked through the chilly dawn with such grim intent.

"Thorbrand might encourage your tongue," was his growled reply. "I do not."

Aelfwynn could admit a few misgivings, then. But surely this would have something to do with Thorbrand's king. Perhaps she had misread Ragnall yesterday. Or had underestimated the fragility of his temper. It was possible he wished to address the way she'd spoken to him...but his choosing to do that off on his own rather than shaming her in front of his whole company was a worry.

When they started into the woods, making a new path across the frozen earth where none had gone before them, her misgivings shifted into something else. Something far sharper.

"We have surely gone too far from the village—" she began, stopping still.

But it was too late. The Northman wrenched her arm, gripping her hard and propelling her in front of him, making it clear he was prepared to drag her through these woods if necessary.

Aelfwynn did not ask where he was taking her again, though her mind raced. For she was suddenly put in the position of having to compare and contrast between kidnappings.

There had been Thorbrand, standing calmly in the middle of the old road, snow all around, quietly letting her know her options. All of them unpleasant. She still shuddered when she thought of it, though not from anything like fear.

And then there was this man, who had a pallor to his sunken cheeks and sour breath. Unlike the rest of the Northmen here, he looked as if he did not spend as much time bathing as they all did. His tunic looked as if he'd used it to catch the better part of his dinner and more, as if he'd slept in it for weeks.

Why should one of Ragnall's men take her? His most slovenly man, for that matter?

But the further away they got from the village, marching through the grim wood, the more her captor began to talk.

"Ragnall is a fool," he seethed at her, his grip harder on her arm as he spoke. "Sending you away when it would be far better to use you now, while your mother's memory still shines bright in Mercia."

No reply from Aelfwynn was necessary, and she thought it a good thing. For what was there to say when his hands were on her? He kept moving, swift and furious, so that she was forced to run to keep up with his bone-rattling pace.

"Your uncle has a Northman problem and we are not going away," the man told her. Or told the trees. Or better still, himself, for he seemed to need no reply from Aelfwynn. "Not in this life. Yet why should Thorbrand get the glory, a kingdom, and an uppity Saxon bride to bear him sons? What has he done that I have not? What, damn you?"

And when Aelfwynn did not answer that, either, his grip tightened, so hard that she could not keep back a yelp. Then, horribly, he shook her—a violent jolt, so hard she fair expected it to separate her head from her neck.

She nearly bit her tongue in half. Pain

bloomed from her nape to the top of her head. And it was all she could do to keep her expression, if not mild, blank enough when he hauled her around to stare down into her face, his sour breath washing over her and making her stomach curdle.

"Answer me that, woman!" he snarled.

"I cannot," she replied calmly. And oh, how it cost her to sound thus. She took the pain and used it. She gazed back at him as if this were any quiet talk in a warm hall, friends and protectors on all sides. "For I do not know you. Tell me your name and your deeds, that I might make a better reckoning."

She realized something else then, there in another cold and inhospitable wood with another man holding her fast. Her lifetime of training had been sound. Mildrithe and her mother had prepared her well. The man who loomed over her now was no different than all the men who had crowded into Tamworth after her mother's death in June. The men who had grabbed her thus, or worse, pretended to support her in public so that she might let her guard down when they came upon her in a quiet corner.

In all cases, she had acquitted herself magnificently, no matter what hopes the Mercians might have had for her that she had dashed. She had exuded calm and carried on saying her prayers, repeat as necessary, until the threat passed her by.

Yet Thorbrand had been different. Because Thorbrand had not made her want to scream. He had seen *her*, whatever else his aims might have been. He had spoken to *her*, not thundered on about his own dreams of Mercian domination or his plans to unseat or cajole her uncle. He had seen her far too clearly, out in that cold night, and had made her choose.

She had been far too besotted with him from the start.

There had been no call to weave her peace when she had wanted nothing more than to lose herself in the sheer heat of his midnight gaze, the glory of his hard hands, and the marvel of his kiss.

With this new, lesser Northman, it was easy enough to adopt her old, familiar posture. Half penitent, half saint. Aelfwynn folded her hands together before her, no matter how awkwardly he held her, so that he could not mistake the evidence of her serene piety even if he preferred his pagan gods to hers. She even gazed back at him, soothingly, and watched as her determined calmness did its work.

Too well did she know that a woman's tears did not always bring out the best in men. Far too many men fed off those tears. Some used them to commit even more desperate acts.

"I am Bjørn," the man told her, pride and rage laced through his voice and the wild gaze he pinned on her. "I fought with Ragnall in Waterford. Have I not followed him since? Have I not slain all manner of enemies? Should my name not be sung? Such was my might at Corbridge last year that some have had it that I won the day."

Aelfwynn's own recollection was that no one knew quite what had happened at the Battle of Corbridge last year. Her mother had claimed victory. But so too had everyone else, particularly Ragnall.

"Why should Thorbrand gather all the spoils because he has known Ragnall the longer?" Bjørn demanded.

"Are they not kin?"

This was clearly the wrong question to ask.

Bjørn scowled at her, his thick blond brows meeting over his eyes. "Thorbrand's father is dead. He has no sons. If he fell tomorrow, who would sing his name were it not for Ragnall's favor? *Who?*"

Aelfwynn discovered something else, then. She did not wish for Thorbrand to fall. She did not wish for the faintest harm to come to him. Even speaking of it so casually made everything in her go rigid, though she knew a warrior such as he would not thank her for such consideration when battle lived in his blood. When it had made him who he was.

Besotted, a voice inside whispered.

She tried to take proper heed of the threat before her. "I will tell you, Bjørn, what I have told Thorbrand already. And indeed your king himself. My uncle considers me no treasure, of this you can be certain. For all the reasons your king wants me in his hands, my uncle wishes me gone forever and, indeed, acted to make it thus. My resurrection will not please him." She considered the man before her, his face mottled and his blond-brown beard in snarls. "I do not think I would wish to be the man who delivers that unsought message to him."

"You speak of politics," Bjørn scoffed. "But what matters is blood. *Your* blood. And I think it more than likely that Edward of Wessex would take it amiss if his niece were paraded through Mercia at the end of a chain. Stripped naked and beaten bloody for all to see. What say you, princess?"

He did not say that word, *princess*, the way Thorbrand did. Aelfwynn did not care for it at all—particularly as she had never been a princess. Funny, was it not, that the accuracy of the term had not concerned her overmuch when it was in Thorbrand's mouth.

But it was better not to think about his mouth. Not here in these ghostly woods, where she couldn't say she was overfond of the way this Bjørn was staring fixedly at hers.

"Indeed he would look ill upon it," Aelfwynn managed to say in the same mild, unassuming manner, though her pulse crowed loud in her ears. "As would any good man who gazed upon a woman treated in so callous a manner, I would hope." Her captor did naught but glare at her, the corners of his mouth wetter than before, and she did not like it at all. She bowed her head. "Let us pray, Bjørn. It is all that sustains me in these darkest days."

Bjørn, unsurprisingly, did not choose to pray with her. He started walking again, shoving her before him as he went. At least that meant he had released his vicious grip on her arm. Aelfwynn advised herself to be grateful for what she could.

And she could not have said how long this went on. When her walking speed was not to Bjørn's taste, he pushed her again—and not gently. Almost as if he wished for her to fall to the cold earth, for reasons she preferred not to consider. Instead, she took it upon herself to pray, loudly.

Yet her melodious Latin only seemed to make Bjørn's muttering sound more and more unhinged the longer they walked away from the village.

The cold morning sun rose as they walked. First it shone through the trees, then it began to filter in from an angle, making the bare branches glow. And Aelfwynn could not allow herself to wonder what it was Thorbrand was doing now. Searching for her, she hoped—

But then, despite all the ways their bodies had become one last night, she had not said she would marry him, had she? She had not reacted at all well to the notion.

He had asked her for her hand, again and again, in their tent last night. Though it had not been so much of an *asking*, in truth. It had been more a part of the rhythm in the way he had thundered between her thighs, wringing her inside out, and then tossing her straight back into the flames.

Over and over, until they were both worn thin with pleasure…

Aelfwynn could not bear the idea that he might think she had left him of her own volition. But she cast that aside even as she thought it. Because he might well believe that, but why should that change a thing for him? Thorbrand had treated her as he had not because he intended to make her a slave, as she had thought he did. But because this was how he intended to take her to wife.

She didn't know how long she walked on, dodging Bjørn's mean-spirited shoves, as she struggled to full take in the meaning of that.

It had been a surprise to her yesterday to discover he wished to marry her. More than simply a surprise—it had made her something like dizzy. Yet it hadn't been a surprise to *him*. He had known all along. He had planned to wed her from the start.

And suddenly everything made a different kind of sense.

The way Thorbrand had handled her from

the beginning. How he had slowly gentled her to his touch, night after night on the road. First the way he had rubbed her down when she ached, then how he had kissed her. How he had draped her over his chest and let her sleep there. And had not, until recently, ever taken her beneath him as he could so easily have done at any point, for she had claimed she disliked it. She thought of the pool where she had given him her maidenhead. More, that he had already been to the cottage before he'd found her on the old road south of Tamworth. He had already known the pool was there— had he waited to rid her of her innocence until they reached it?

Aelfwynn was no fool and now no innocent, either. And thus she knew that he could have taken her at any time and not concerned himself much with her pleasure while he was about it. For she understood now, in retrospect, the women's talk she'd overheard before. Words she had heard and thought little of meant different things to her now that she, too, was as delightfully sinful as anyone else.

She remembered, at the start, fearing that Thorbrand might simply take what he wanted from her. She had worried he would glut himself and then give her to his brother and cousin. And she could not have said when it was she had stopped worrying about those things, only that she had—and that before they had arrived at the cottage. Because all along, Thorbrand had kept her safe. He had fed her. He had warmed her. He had cared for her—rubbing out the aches in her body and claiming only kisses in return.

Kisses. She stumbled over an up-thrust root on the forest floor and caught herself, darting a glance back to see the way Bjørn lunged forward—then stopped when she remained upright.

No, indeed, she told herself stoutly. *I shall not fall.*

Aelfwynn kept on, though her mind still raced. How had she possibly imagined that the way Thorbrand had treated her was how a man treated a slave? One he might choose to sell or brutalize or both? A concubine he could do with as he wished, including have her sacrificed upon his death, if she had heard the stories true?

Even when he had chased off her men and swung up behind her on that poor old nag, it had been a far kinder, respectful affair than this. She knew well that even a properly chosen bride sent off to a new house with every promise made, from the *handgeld* given in payment to the bride's family to the price of the *brýdgifu* a woman took with her and kept as her own even should her husband perish—all hammered out to the satisfaction of the two families involved in the customary way—might not fare as well as she had done with a Northman who'd laid in wait for her in the road. For there were many things supposedly frowned upon inside the walls of a warm hall where all was pleasant and bright, but that did not prevent them happening. Sometimes right outside the walls. Sometimes in the shadows there within.

And she knew, in the part of her deep inside that had always wanted to fight like her mother, that Bjørn had no intention of treating her with anything like the steel-tipped kindness Thorbrand had showed her. Rather the opposite—and she was glad of it that he walked behind her so he could not see how she failed to keep her countenance smooth and untroubled in that moment.

Aelfwynn tried to quiet her mind. She marched on and on, the ground beneath her feet either frozen solid where the woods were thick, or muddy when the sun's light shone through. She was cold and her belly was empty, but on she marched.

Deep within, she believed that Thorbrand would search for her. That did not mean he would find her. And even if he did, he might not do so before she was forced to suffer through any number of indignities at this Bjørn's hands.

Aelfwynn was pleased, then, that this morning before she'd exited the tent she had opened the pouches she'd taken with her from Tamworth and found the dagger that Thorbrand had confiscated. The first time he had pulled her underdress to her waist and put his hands on her body as he pleased, their second night together. She could not have said what, exactly, had inspired her to seek out the dagger when she had not thought of it since he'd taken it from her. A mixture of uncertainty and temper, were she honest with herself. Uncertainty about what her future held, whether as a wife to Northman or even as a bride in this village where there were only strangers and none of her family or friends. And temper because Thorbrand's announcement that he intended to marry her had infuriated her. It had wrecked her. It had made her feel too many things she had not the words to describe.

But this was not the time to sort through her feelings.

Bjørn kept muttering as they moved on through the woods. She thought again of the unpleasant blast of his sour breath on her face and realized she should have known at once that he had partaken of far more than his share of mead. Had been up all night with it, if she had to hazard a guess. She had seen the like before on too many mornings to count. Who had not who lived in halls with men who preferred a full cup to courage?

Aelfwynn could feel the dagger concealed at her waist, safely beneath her cloak, as she walked. And she took comfort in its presence there. She needed only wait for the right moment to use it, and would. She could still feel the ache in her neck from when Bjørn had shaken her and knew she would have no trouble wielding a blade.

The truth was, she had felt safer in Thorbrand's hands than she ever had anywhere else. How had she not recognized it? *How would you know safety?* she asked herself then. *When have you experienced it?* She missed her mother dreadfully. She suspected she always would, as all children missed their parents when they died, no matter that it was the way of things. But her mother had concerned herself with war. Fighting and bloodshed without end.

Aelfwynn had either been by her side or left behind somewhere, waiting for word.

She had disliked both. Neither had been *safe*.

Safe was a gift. Only Thorbrand had ever given it to her.

As the morning wore on, Aelfwynn found a kind of rhythm in the walking. It made her think of the cottage. The simplicity of a day arranged around how food was made, and when. Though all days were structured in this way, Aelfwynn had never been the one to oversee the tasks that needed doing. The days in the cottage had a beginning, when she woke. And an end, when Thorbrand laid her out before him near the fire or tumbled her into the furs, and she thought no more of domestic tasks until morning. Each day was the same and yet not the same. There was a pleasure in the making of things. A joy and satisfaction in preparing food and drink that would sustain them both. And the reward that came every time he touched her.

If she married him, she could see very clearly, that would be their life. A simple, beautiful, shared life of rhythm and structure.

Until such a time as his king called him back. And then they would return to these wars, these bloody battlefields, these games men played when kingdoms were in the offing. Yesterday she had thought it an impossibility. How could she marry him and live as they had in the cottage, forever knowing a call could come at any time? And that the call must be answered as a matter of honor? It was too cruel.

But here in these woods, captive once more and in a way that boded only ill, she rather thought it would be worth it. However long she could spend with Thorbrand, in the life they made to suit themselves, it would be worth it.

As she thought that, she knew something else. She would do whatever was necessary to get away from this drunken oaf, because she wanted the sweetness and simple joy of that cottage once again. Even if it were only for a season. A mere breath between battles. It would still be more safety, more happiness, than she had ever known.

Love, a voice inside her said. That perilous word.

You may love Mercia, Aethelflaed had said when Aelfwynn had gathered up her courage one day when she was yet a girl and had asked her mother if she might not consider a love match for her only daughter. *You may love Mercia as hard and as deep as you can, daughter. You will need no other love match.* And her gaze, so much like Aelfwynn's own, had been steady when it met hers. *For no other love match will you make. Though if you are lucky and if you dedicate yourself to the task as if were a military campaign, you will find that any match can be made over to suit you.*

Her answer had not surprised Aelfwynn, necessarily. She had witnessed her parents' union. She had seen it with her own eyes when her mother had ascended to rule Mercia after her husband's death. Still. *Some are permitted to love. Why should I be denied it?*

It is a silly girl who loves the men that court

*her with pretty words and gold-bright prom-
ises,* Aethelflaed had told her, in a voice soft
for so strong a lady. *But a wise wife who takes
her time and the measure of the hall before
offering the same.*

Here, in these cold woods, Aelfwynn
smiled fondly where Bjørn could not see her.

*I have never wanted your kingdoms,
Mother,* she said quietly inside. To a pair of
steady gold eyes like hers. *But I will fight all
the same for the simple pleasures of a cottage.*

And so she waited. She walked as carefully
as she could, not wanting a twisted ankle to
make the situation worse. If such a thing were
possible. On and on they walked, until the sun
hit its midday peak, not very high at all this
time of year. And Aelfwynn tensed when the
man behind her slowed.

"We will rest here," he told her. "Mayhap
I'll take a turn at what Thorbrand has had full
access to first."

Vile pig.

Aelfwynn turned to face him, for she might
not be a warrior queen like her mother, but she
was no coward. "Do you not fear that Thorbrand is on your trail, even now?"

"You think highly of yourself," Bjørn

sneered. Then made a show of tossing off the cloak he wore and fumbling at the fastening of his trousers. "Your charms must be great indeed."

What was there for Aelfwynn to do but stand still? And prepare herself. She wrapped her arms around her middle, hoping he would mistake it for frailty. When instead she gripped the hilt of her dagger. *Steady,* she told herself. *You may only have the opportunity to strike but once.*

"Thorbrand may rejoice to find you gone," Bjørn told her. He did not pull out his male flesh, for which she was grateful, but the threat of it seemed to loom large over the small, cold clearing she found herself in.

"He might indeed," Aelfwynn agreed in as serene a manner as she could manage. "But that would not change, I think, his king's directives. And the king is who we serve, do we not?"

"Not you, little traitor." Bjørn's scowl took over his face. He took a step toward her. "You are Edward of Wessex's niece, the daughter of the Lady of the Mercians, reduced to nothing but a Northman's *hōra.* And yet you look no worse for wear. Your uncle wanted you dead when you sought a blameless nunnery. What will he do to you when he learns the breadth of your other talents? When I tell him?"

He staggered closer, and though he was wiry and pale, he was yet a man. Bigger than her and no stranger to battle. She gripped her knife harder and held herself still.

"What I don't understand," Aelfwynn said quietly, very deliberately, "is why, in all of these scenes you have made up to amuse yourself, you imagine that you, a ragged-looking Northman who smells of drink, will stride forward to engage King Edward of Wessex in casual conversation. Where would this take place? When would it happen? You will be shot dead by a thousand arrows before you make it a day's walk into Mercia. You will never, ever reach his side."

The sneer on Bjørn's face seemed to elongate, then turn into a nightmare. "Then I had better make sure to take my taste now, *tík.*"

With that slur hanging in the air, likening her to a female dog, he lunged at her. But Aelfwynn was ready. She did not try to slash at him or engage in any of the complicated knife maneuvers she'd seen men perform while they practiced for war. All Aelfwynn did was hold her hands before her as if in prayer. But with the blade up.

So when Bjørn reached for her to haul her against him and hurt her, he cut himself.

He howled, staggering back.

Now did Aelfwynn hold the blade the way she had seen men do. High before her, in the hope that the next time he ran at her she could do yet more damage.

"Niðingr!" he roared at her, calling her yet another name, this one deeming her less than a person. A nothing. A *thing*. "Little *tík*!"

He slapped a hand on the place where she'd cut him on his arm, his palm coming away red with his own blood. And she watched the man in him, what little there was, leave him. His eyes went flat. His lip curled.

If she died here, Aelfwynn thought resolutely, she would do so as gracefully as she could—and she would leave him in ribbons first.

He lunged at her again, but she darted to one side, holding the knife before her. She dared not look away from his twisted, furious face. She hardly dared breathe. For she knew that now, having seen her knife and felt its sting, he would go for it first. Aelfwynn intended to make sure it cost him.

They circled each other in the clearing, and Aelfwynn felt far too many things rise up within her, one feeling after the next she dared not entertain. Not now. If she survived, if she lived another day, she could entertain all the feelings she wished.

Bjørn stopped moving, clearly recalculating the situation. Aelfwynn stopped moving too, aware that her chest was heaving as if she'd been breathing heavily all along. Perhaps she had been. She found she did not know.

The wood all around them was quiet. The cold winter sun hardly cleared the bare tops of the trees, heedless and uncaring. Aelfwynn shifted her grip on the dagger, and warned herself to prepare to fight, for none would save her. She must save herself, and so she would.

She yet had that much of Aethelflaed within her.

Harder she gripped the dagger, and this time, she intended to swing—

"I see I will have to teach you how to wield a blade, sweeting," came a dark, low, wonderfully familiar voice from the edge of the clearing. But Aelfwynn dared not take her eyes off

Bjørn. Not yet. Not before she knew whether or not she was dreaming. "Though from the looks of it, you have already hit your mark. Which is more than you can say, Bjørn, you mewling *rassragr.*"

Aelfwynn didn't have to know what the word meant to know it was a vile insult. Because Bjørn threw back his head and let out a kind of howl. Frustration. Rage. But it was not until he turned to face Thorbrand that Aelfwynn did too.

She had never been more pleased to see a man. To see *this* man.

Thorbrand stood at the edge of the clearing, looking bored, though he was dressed for war, his shield at the ready and his sword in his hand. Bored, that was, until she looked closer at the way his dark blue eyes blazed. Hot and bright with fury she had never seen before. His gaze raked over her, then dismissed her, returning to Bjørn. And darkening.

Which was as well, for all Aelfwynn wanted to do was drink in the sight of him.

Her wild Northman warrior, who regarded her captor as if he were a field mouse he'd caught in a trap and now intended to bat about, then slay without a second thought.

"Why should the spoils go to you?" Bjørn howled at him. "I have fought at Ragnall's side the better part of a decade. Why should you be chosen?"

"I can think of a great number of reasons," Thorbrand replied in a harsh voice Aelfwynn had never heard from him before. And she was not so gentle as she wished she was, for the sound thrilled her. He was powerful beyond measure, and he wished to marry her. She flushed slightly and knew it to be pleasure. "But first, I do not stand in the middle of a forest in winter with my pants at my knees and my dick in the wind."

"I will kill you for these insults," Bjørn whispered, so pale with fury his beard shook. "I will wear your ribs as a helmet."

"I believe he has had too much of the drink," Aelfwynn felt compelled to state. "He is not well."

"Ah, but you do not know our Bjørn." Thorbrand stepped into the clearing and faced the other man, though his body was loose. He sheathed his sword and tossed his shield aside, then looked as if he'd relaxed completely. As if he thought there was no threat here. Aelfwynn blinked, then realized this, too, was an insult.

"Always the last to volunteer and the first to complain. The quickest to charge into battle when the king is watching, yet less quick toward his own death when left to his own devices. No injury too small to be nursed forever. No boast too large, yet too little to back it up. Bjørn is no warrior. He is a boy who never learned how to be a man."

"This boy will make you eat those words," Bjørn bellowed, pulling free his sword, and then charging.

Aelfwynn sucked in a breath, expecting Thorbrand to reach for his own sword again—

But he didn't. He merely watched the other man's attack as if it was happening slowly. As if he had all the time in the world. Then, just before Bjørn's sword should surely have cleaved his head in two he stepped to one side and somehow, with a quick, fluid motion Aelfwynn could not comprehend, both relieved Bjørn of his sword, and sent the other man sprawling to the cold ground.

"I have a better idea," Thorbrand said, in a quiet fury that Aelfwynn could feel inside her, like heat. "I will leave you to eat your own sword."

And then he lifted it as if to pierce the other man straight through where he lay.

"Thorbrand." Aelfwynn gasped out his name. "Not while he lives. Defenseless before you. Where is the honor in that?"

It seemed to take a very long while for Thorbrand to lift his gaze to her. When he did, the blaze in his eyes was so intense that Aelfwynn took a step backward and nearly dropped her dagger. "Yes, Aelfwynn, let us protect the man who would even now be glutting himself on your body had I not arrived when I did."

She didn't understand the fury she could plainly see in him, still, though Bjørn had been laid flat upon the earth. Yet her chin seemed to lift of its own accord as she aimed a cool gaze at Thorbrand in return.

"I have not asked you to protect him. I merely thought you might not sully yourself with a death like this on your hands, when surely, it would be better if he explained himself to his king and accepted the judgment owed him."

For Ragnall, she was sure, would not give a creature who stole from him an easy death.

Thorbrand studied her for a moment, then

flipped the sword he held, bringing the hilt down, and hard, against Bjørn's head. So the other man lolled there as if dead, though Aelfwynn could see his breath on the air.

"Now, Aelfwynn," Thorbrand said, in a pleasant voice completely belied by the thunderous look he threw at her. "Perhaps you can tell me why it is you calmly walked away from the village with this man on the very day we are to wed. Looking, by all accounts, more than happy to accompany him. Into the dark forest."

And now his voice was scathing. *"Alone."*

Chapter Thirteen

Det som göms i snö, kommer fram vid tö.

What is hidden in snow, is revealed at thaw.
—Old Nordic Proverb

Thorbrand wanted to tear Bjørn apart. He wanted to make him an example, a monument of blood and pain to make it clear to all living men, everywhere, that Thorbrand would tolerate no hand on his woman save his own. Ever.

He was not entirely certain he wouldn't still do precisely that.

And maybe in so doing, appease the gods— and his father's memory—for the woman he had not protected once before.

But Aelfwynn stood before him, still clutching her dagger with her golden eyes bright and mutinous. And his heart beat so hard it jarred his ribs, but though she looked dirtier than was usual—mud splattered all over her gown, her hair a wild snarl, and high color on her cheeks—he could detect no signs of ill use. She did not look hurt. She did not even look afraid.

It was the only reason Bjørn yet drew breath.

For were there so much as the faintest bruise upon her, or any hint of fear or sorrow on her lovely brow, and he would have killed the man where he lay. Defenseless or not, it would have made no difference.

"Do you plan to answer me, then?" he growled at her, Bjørn incapacitated and therefore of no more interest to him.

Aelfwynn's chin rose higher and it called to his blood. It fair sang for her, damn her. "I thought he was taking me to your king."

"Does my king spend his mornings lurking about in Northumbrian woods, then? That is new."

"I have heard tell he might indeed be part troll." She only looked demure when he scowled at that insult. "He has quite a reputation, Thorbrand. I assumed he cultivated such himself."

"Ragnall might kill a troll or twenty and consider it a lazy morning," Thorbrand said darkly, not at all sure why he was debating *trolls*, "but what he would never do is send a depraved weakling to handle a woman who was important enough he dispatched three of his best men to spirit her away from Mercia to begin with."

"If Bjørn is so disgraceful a warrior, why did he come here with your king anyway? Surely accompanying Ragnall on a journey is a coveted position. Available to only the strongest and best men, handpicked for their valor and honor alike."

"There is nothing to say that Bjørn was expected to return from this journey. The wolves are hungry in winter, and better a small man provide them a meal than a king. Or you or me." He shook his head. "Three villagers tending to the cattle saw you, Aelfwynn. Merrily wandering off into the woods. No hand upon you, no knife at your back."

"I would hardly call the way I walked into uncertainty *merry*. Or anything like a *wander*, come to that."

"Do you deny this is what you did?"

"How was I to know what he had in mind?" Aelfwynn asked, sounding exasperated. With him, if Thorbrand was not mistaken. She huffed out a breath. "As far as I was aware, he was a chosen warrior bound to Ragnall's side. Why should I not imagine he came for me on an errand for his king? In case it has escaped your attention, I am not one of you. Your king only yesterday was happy enough to speak of potentially killing me should he wish it. And I make a habit to be as accommodating as possible when around men who wish to kill me, Thorbrand. You should know this well. It is why at least two kings have plotted my death in recent memory, yet I live."

He found he did not like the way she said that, though he had said something similar to her. Much less the way she looked at him as she spoke.

"Perhaps," he gritted out, "you should stop these games altogether. There are good manners and then there is idiocy."

"Is there indeed?" she asked, her voice sweet. Though what lay beneath it was not. It was an edge far sharper than that of the dagger yet in her hand and he could feel it as if she'd cut him. "What a novel concept. I should simply *stop accommodating* the great many men who storm into my path and insist I bend to their superior will. What would have been my fate, I wonder, if after my mother died I had opted not to flatter anyone or behave in the least bit subservient or agreeable? If I had rashly picked a side. Chosen the path *I* wanted without concerning myself with anyone else's wishes. Given myself to one of my suitors. Done as I pleased, for once."

He liked hearing about her *suitors* even less than hearing that edge in her voice. "Worry less about fate, for it will find you no matter what you do."

"I would be dead, Thorbrand," she tossed back at him. "Killed as a traitor to my uncle or as a disappointment to Mercia. Killed because I could only ever be a symbol to any of them, of what had already been lost. Do you truly believe that it could be otherwise?"

"And yet you were not concerned about accommodating me overly when your life was in my hands, were you?" Thorbrand had spent so long with this woman, yet constrained. Forced to hold himself back for one reason or another. But now they stood in yet another frozen wood and a man who had dared take what was his at their feet. She would be his wife before nightfall, no matter what she might have told herself to the contrary. He feared he had no restraint left within him. Or perhaps the truth was that he did not *fear* that at all when it felt far more like freedom. "Or was that what you wanted, Aelfwynn? Better for a Saxon *symbol* to die at the savage Northman's hands. Think of what they would whisper about you if you were taken, yet lived to tell the tale."

And to his astonishment—and though he admitted it only to himself, his deep and dark delight—she actually brandished the dagger she held at him.

At him.

Like a woman of ferocity who could handle anything, even him.

Especially him.

There were bright northern summers in her gaze, reminding him of lands where the sun never set. There was a glorious fury on her face. And Thorbrand had never seen any so beautiful as this woman. He had never wanted any woman more, so much that he resented his own king for the interest he had in her.

He wanted to rip these feelings out of himself and burn them on a fire.

Failing that, he would settle for burning the two of them alive in a manner that brought him far more satisfaction, for all that it was never, ever enough.

Nor will it ever be, something in him spoke. Like prophecy.

But Aelfwynn thrust her dagger forward as if she meant to thrust it straight through his chest. More than once.

And Thorbrand could have disarmed her easily, but did not. Because he liked this side of his woman. He had wanted to tear down the hills at the thought he'd lost her today. And tearing down hills was the least he would have done had he found her foully abused by the likes of Bjørn. There could have been no price paid that could have assuaged him.

Yet he still wanted to see where she went with a dagger and that temper in her gaze.

He craved it.

"I have spent my entire life making certain that I'm nothing but agreeable and accommodating at all costs," she threw at him. "By the time you condescended to stop me on that road, I had already exhausted myself making certain that any who ventured near me in the wake of my mother's death thought only of my serene countenance. My endless prayers. And my blameless character, inoffensive to all."

"And thus you are known throughout the land. Do you wish me to congratulate you on this? Or do you not realize that being known as such is an insult?"

"It were no accident, Thorbrand!" she threw at him. "How do you think I survived?"

"Because of your blood," he replied, frowning because the question was foolish. Did she truly require his answer? "What else?"

She moved closer, still brandishing her little blade. Again, he could have taken it from her, but what would be the fun in that? Far better to see where she was headed, to his mind. What she was capable of when she wasn't pretending to be one of her saints.

"Let me tell you something about my blood," she seethed at him, a ferocious expression on her face that made him as hard as it did happy, though he would not have admitted the latter. She need not know how he craved her. How he longed for a wildness to match his own, particularly as his future battles would like as not take place mostly in their bed. He wanted a worthy opponent and he had known that she had this in her. He had tasted it. "It is all well and good to claim a direct line from King Alfred, all praise his name, but what good does it do me? Were I my mother's son, who can say what might have happened? My mother might never have ruled at all. But I was born a daughter. And thus all my royal blood has ever done for me is make me a target. A prize. A bit of tender to be bartered between men as they decide what sort of treaty I might become. All I ever wanted to do was fight, Thorbrand, and so I did—though you may disdain my weapons."

"I do not disdain your weapons," he replied, impatiently. She waved that dagger at him again, and he could not tell if she wished to stick him with it or if she'd forgotten she even held it. "Though I tire, Aelfwynn, of that sharp little blade too close to my face."

She frowned at the knife as if she'd never seen it before, but once again lifted her gaze back to him. Her frown deepened. And he could see that a great emotion held her fast. Her bodice heaved with the force of it. Her cheeks blazed with heat.

He found her almost too beautiful to bear,

especially in high color and her version of fury crackling through her. He wanted her beneath him. He *wanted* her and she had walked off into the woods with a man who might have hurt her, or killed her, and he did not see himself forgetting that any time soon.

"Every woman knows the fates that await her, no matter how blameless," she told him. She made a faint sound, not quite a laugh. "The veil is a gift accorded the few."

Aelfwynn shook slightly as she said that and he did not know if it was because she still longed for her nunnery. Something he might have to take as a personal insult if she did not cease—not that it would change her destiny. Nothing could.

And that was not because of the gods but because Thorbrand had no intention of letting her slip away from him again. Ever.

"You may think it foolish to concern yourself with a destiny when it has already been decided, but women are different, are they not?" Her eyes were like flame, the dagger still aimed at his throat. "Men can rely on fate. Women must rely on men, and of the two, I warrant fate is the kinder."

"Then you know it little."

She ignored his words. "A woman may be a wife or concubine. Free or a slave. But no matter what she becomes, often through no fault or choice of her own, the work of it remains the same. Men are to be flattered. Supported. Obeyed and admired in all things. I was yet a girl when I learned that my mother was permitted to do things no other woman could. But why? Not because she wished it alone. But because it suited her husband to *allow her* to do those things. As it suited her brother, who *let her* do as she wished. My father died before he could marry me to a rival or an enemy, but my uncle did not waste his time putting me in my place. I am left to wonder if my mother never knew her power had been borrowed all the while."

"Life is hard and short, sweeting," Thorbrand rumbled at her. "I have spent mine on one long, endless military campaign where who has power and who does not is always readily apparent in who lives and who dies. What else is there? Men must take or be taken, that is the way of the world. Better learn to swing a sword or you will find yourself flattened by another's." He shrugged. "I chose to swing mine, and well."

"I congratulate you on having a choice at all."

Thorbrand studied her, that frown on her face and the dagger yet extended. Her chest was still rising and falling rapidly, making him wonder why they were standing thus, when this was a conversation better had naked.

As he thought all conversations with this woman should be had.

"What is it that irks you?" he asked her. Her eyes flashed and she opened her mouth, but he shook his head. "I do not wish to hear another story about your family or the trials of your bloodline. It was only you and me in that hall yesterday. I told you I meant to marry you and you reacted poorly. Why?"

Her hand trembled as she held on to her dagger. But for a moment, all was silent save the sound of her ragged breathing. The winter wind had picked up slightly, rattling through the branches up above them. Yet he could smell the earth beneath them, muddy and wet, and in the rich scent of it, the promise of green things. Months hence, but still. A promise all the same.

"You should have told me you meant to

marry me from the start," she said quietly, and her eyes seemed big. Overbright. "I thought I was your slave."

"That you were wrong should fill you with joy, should it not?" His voice was dry. "It should not inspire you to swing a dagger in my direction, I would have thought."

"You should have told me," she said again, more intensely. And that gleam in her gaze even brighter than before. "I do not think you would take it lightly if you thought your freedom have been taken from you, do you? Better to know."

"But what freedom of yours did I take?" he asked, and it was an effort to keep his voice calm when he would have preferred to roar. To thunder at her about that dagger and her foolishness and whatever else would end this standoff and get her in his arms, where she belonged. "Have you not been at pains to tell me what few choices women have? Whether you call yourself a wife or a thrall, you belong to another. To me, Aelfwynn. Why should it matter to you which, if you are already as constrained as you claim?"

The dagger moved even closer. "There is a difference between a wife and a slave!"

"Not for you," Thorbrand said, dark and low. "We have already had a taste of it, have we not? If you believed yourself a slave, it is a certainty you were not ill-used. I dare you to claim otherwise."

"Do you think that makes it any better? For I may assure you it does not."

"I will tell you what I think," Thorbrand told her, and he moved closer to her then, until, had he breathed in too deeply, he would scrape himself with the pointed end of her blade. He glared down at her, somehow keeping his hands at his sides when he wanted nothing more than to touch her. To haul her close. To show her how they fit, as she'd apparently forgotten. "You would rather be my thrall."

Aelfwynn gasped. "I would rather no such thing! No freeborn person would ever wish for such shame!"

He pushed on, ignoring her outburst. "That way, you can carry on as you have, forever congratulating yourself on your martyrdom. Is that not what fuels your pious little Christian soul? Your great sacrifice. Your struggle."

There were too many emotions to name, then, crowding through her eyes like gold. He noted each and every one of them, though he could not have named them.

Thorbrand leaned closer to her, flirting with the point of that knife. "But if you are my wife, Aelfwynn, what then? If you are not martyring yourself to the Northman beast, could it be that this is not the great sacrifice you would prefer it to be? That you are not suffering, after all? Because try though you might, you cannot escape what you feel, can you? And worse, what you want."

She had gone still. Pale. "You have no idea what I want."

"You want me," he roared at her, and liked it too well when she jumped at that. And better still, flushed bright red, telling him the truths her skin knew, even if she denied it. "But the notion offends your Mercian sensibilities, so far better, in your mind, that you succumb to a terrible fate than that I marry you and protect you and live out a life with you. By the gods, you would rather come to me in chains."

"I have done no choosing and I want no chains," Aelfwynn said, though she sounded very nearly stricken, the dagger dropping to her side. "Yet you would wed me just as you took me in the first place, whether I chose it or no."

Thorbrand eyed her. "Did I not give you a choice on the eve when first we met?"

"Yes, and a fine choice it was. Wolves, bandits, men set to rip me to pieces around the next bend...or you."

He laughed. "There is always a choice. What you want are choices you find agreeable, sweeting, and those are not gifts the gods tend to bestow. Better learn that now, when, like it or do not, none of the choices you have made will kill you. Many are not so lucky."

"I should have risked the wolves," she threw at him. "They could only have been easier to reason with than you."

Thorbrand leaned to put his face close to hers, and he was not laughing any longer. "You will never escape me, Aelfwynn. The wolves cannot have you. But mark this. You can decide, here and now, whether our marriage be a pleasure or a prison."

And he watched as she stood there before him in this cold clearing, shaking from the force of the emotions that swept over her, too many waves on an unquiet sea. He saw the fight in her and, at her side, the way her hand that still held that dagger trembled.

But he knew her too well. His little martyr. His woebegone saint.

"What galls you is not that I meant to marry you from the start," he said, and did not hide the dark laughter that moved in him. "But that, were you my slave indeed, you would have loved the role all the same."

And maybe he should have expected that look of surprise on her face. Then the bright bloom of color that followed, something too complicated to be simply temper. Shame, perhaps. That fire that was theirs, that burned even now.

But she stopped shaking.

"You are a demon straight from hell," she bit out.

"And that is how you like me, Aelfwynn," he replied, not in the least insulted. "Over and over again. Night and day."

Her eyes were too bright with all of those things he could see tracking over her lovely face. She was not the least bit serene. He had never seen her thus, a bright, burning flame of temper.

She was a vision. Even when she swung that dagger, and cut him.

It was a slice across his forearm, little more than a scratch—but she'd *cut him*. She'd blooded him.

For a long, tense, exhilarating moment, they only stared at each other. Aelfwynn's jaw dropped open with what looked like shock. While Thorbrand's whole body tightened with an outrage mixed with need, a bright hot flame that he was not certain he would survive.

He was not sure he *wished* to survive it.

And when Aelfwynn turned and ran for the trees, he laughed loud and long.

Then chased her.

Chapter Fourteen

Sob hit sylf acybeð.

Truth will make itself known.

—*The Durham Proverbs*

Aelfwynn threw herself through the trees, desperate to get away.

Desperate to escape.

His terrible words, ripping her open wide. The horror of the things he'd said, like arrows striking her through the heart. She told herself he was wrong. She told herself he knew not the dark places inside her, the things she dared not speak aloud.

He was *wrong.* Her mother had been Aethelflaed, Lady of the Mercians. She was granddaughter to King Alfred. She wanted to be no man's thrall. Her very blood forbade it.

She ran in a blind panic, wanting nothing but to put space between her and the Northman who had spoken her deepest, most awful truths out loud. She cared not that branches caught at her, that roots seemed to rise up to trip her—

But a strong arm caught her, hauling her back, before the latest roots laid her out on the forest floor.

And Aelfwynn had the clear thought that there was no further need for her to be quite so obliging. Or accommodating. Or in any way *agreeable*, thank you. Not to this man who had flayed her open with such thunderous deliberation.

So she fought.

For the first time in her whole life, Aelfwynn fought not with her words and her silences, her prayers and her piety. She did not smile. She was not *serene*.

Finally, she fought.

Thorbrand held her against him, his arms around her like bands of steel. He laughed while her arms flailed and her legs followed suit, seeming not to feel it at all when her heels landed blows or her fists found purchase.

He seemed not to feel it and so she struggled harder, screaming out her fury and her *feelings* to the sullen winter sky.

"Go on then," he urged her at her ear. "Exhaust yourself."

Aelfwynn hated that he knew. That he knew far too much. That he knew the darkness in her heart and the longing in her body. That he knew, even before she did, what she longed for. What she truly longed for.

She had always imagined it was this battle.

Bravely did she fight on, but she already knew she was lost. She already knew that writhing about in his arms was nothing but a frustration. For she knew too well a different struggle. The two of them wrapped up tight in his furs, fighting to get closer, to get deeper, to lose themselves forever in the slick, sweet heat that had become as dear to Aelfwynn as breathing.

But she had always told herself that if given the chance, she would fight the way men did, all fists and blades and savage cries of dominance. So she kept going, even though the more she fought, the more a new, more unpalatable truth wormed its way into her.

I do not wish to fight him, she acknowledged, though it hurt. *I would fight* for *him. I would fight* with *him.*

Yet the truth she least wanted to face was what he'd said before she'd wielded her dagger at last. She had thought herself his slave and had still loved her time in that cottage. She had found a deep joy in the quiet rhythm of a life finally shared. There had been no distance between them, for how could there have been? They might tend to different tasks, but both had been in service of the same ends. Food and shelter and a fire to keep them warm.

For once, Aelfwynn had not been set apart. For once, she had known a real intimacy that she had only heard tell of, before. Not only the things he did to her that made her shudder so and call out his name. But the fabric of their days, stitched together unevenly for she was no deft hand with a needle, but only theirs.

Like a secret, she thought now, but not because she would have tried to hide it had others been near. But because it belonged to them alone. The rhythm and the sweetness. All theirs.

And because she loved him. Slave or wife. Lady or thrall. She loved him all the same.

Had she fallen in love with him the very

first moment she'd seen him standing in the road, covered in dark and snow?

She sagged against him, undone. Her breath was coming in high-pitched now, almost wheezing, so fiercely had she fought him. Aelfwynn thought she could be proud of that, at least. That she had fought as hard as she could.

Thorbrand turned her around in his arms, still holding her off the ground, and then flattened her back against the nearest tree.

"You drew my blood," he growled at her, and she had never seen him look so dark. So thoroughly stern.

It should have terrified her, but it did not. Instead, it seemed to set her aflame. Until it was as if her heart became lodged between her legs, sending out waves of need until her whole body burned the same.

Hot and bright and never-ending.

"You seem no worse for wear," she managed to say.

"I will allow it," he said with all his usual arrogance, as if she had not spoken. "We will consider it a wedding gift, you and I. But were I you, Aelfwynn, I would think carefully before you lift a blade to me again. Very, very carefully."

"Thorbrand—" she began.

She was furious. She was desperate. *She loved him.*

And she yearned for something she dared not name, for she had been taught better. There were no love matches for her. No love matches between a Northman and the woman he had abducted out of her uncle's keeping, however indifferent that keeping might have been. She was foolish to imagine otherwise.

Yet imagine otherwise she did.

His mouth was on hers then, and that fire that ever roared between them swept over her. Like a glorious fever and she welcomed it. She longed for more even as it took her over.

And Aelfwynn didn't think. She did not worry over how best to handle him, or what she ought to do with her expression, her gaze, *her.*

She simply met his kiss with all the fury she felt inside. All the shame. All the need and the fear and the panic he brought out in her, all that heavy and overwhelming love, because he saw her.

He had seen her from the start.

He had seen her plain when she had grown so accustomed to disappearing while others gazed upon her that it had never occurred to her that anyone could look at her and truly *see* her. Not her grandfather. Not her parents. Not her powerful uncle.

They had seen a useful tool. A favored child who would nonetheless find her true calling only when she married for strategic purposes. Or in Edward's case, a minor inconvenience to be removed from the inevitable sweep of his rule.

Thorbrand might have wanted to use her name for his benefit, but that was a name. He yet saw her as a woman. He treated her first and foremost as a woman.

As his woman.

She had never been simply… Aelfwynn.

Until now.

And as if to prove it, Thorbrand ate her alive.

He hauled her up high, shoving her dress and underdress out of his way. Then he tore her hose down to her ankles so he could raise her knees up on either side of his body. He freed himself in the same rush, and then he slammed himself home.

Aelfwynn shattered at once, the pleasure so intense and the fit so thick and full, that it was all she could do to throw back her head and let out a long, keening cry. Of joy. Of surrender. Of love.

Thorbrand gave her no quarter. He thrust into her again and again, that glorious pounding, as if he, too, had thought her lost to him. As if he regarded that loss in the same way she did.

As if the very notion of any separation between them was unbearable.

He put his mouth at her ear, working himself into the slick grasp of her body again and again.

"If you wish to rant at me about the trials of this life of ours, you may do so only when we are joined thus," he growled, fierce and hot. "If you wish to try to cut me, use your nails and no dagger. We will all play our parts in the future laid out for us, that is a certainty, but you and I? We will always meet here, Aelfwynn. We will always meet right here."

"Thorbrand…" she managed to say.

But only that. Only his name.

And then she was shattering all over again,

sharper and wilder than before, and this time, he went with her.

Until there was nothing but the joining.

And the joy that was only theirs, and only this.

Thorbrand held her there for some time, both of them lost the wildness of their breath and when he pulled out of her, she let out a soft sigh of disappointment. For then, again, they were two once more. She felt the cold of the day. The stretch in her thighs. The places she'd kicked against rocks and roots as she'd run, as she'd been shoved, making her feet feel tender. The way she melted still despite these things.

He set her down gently and she busied herself pulling her hose back into place. Then smoothing down her dresses and trying her best to put her cloak to rights. Though she dared not run a hand over her hair, afraid of the damage she might find.

Maybe part of her hoped she yet looked as wild as she felt.

As wild as he'd made her.

"You will marry me this day," Thorbrand told her then as he fastened his trousers, his voice all command. "I will hear you say it."

"I will marry you," she agreed. She did not have to consider it. "This day."

And it could have been an eternity that passed then, his midnight blue gaze hard on hers. The feeling of him still between her thighs. The longing that never left her. Always empty, then, yet always full.

Joy, something in her whispered. *Love.*

No one had told her she should anticipate either. They had told her to live up to their legends, and so she would, if not as they'd imagined. She would fight to love a wild and savage Northman and should they find themselves in Mercia again, she would not hide it.

Aelfwynn did not intend to hide her true self again. Not ever.

"I did not expect this," Thorbrand said then, his voice quiet, but rough. He moved to wrap his hands around her shoulders, tilting her so that she had no choice but to meet his gaze. To lose herself in all that intent dark blue. Even if, given the choice, she would have done exactly this. "I did not expect *you*, Aelfwynn."

That hurt, as if he'd cut her in return, and she did not have it in her to hide it as she ought.

To lower her gaze, to smile. To disappear again. "I apologize if I am a disappointment."

She ought to have been well used to the feeling, after her half year of pleasing no one as the potential new Lady of the Mercians. It was worse now. She had thought then only of surviving, yet with Thorbrand, she wanted so much more.

So very much more, it made her breathless.

But she had learned something very important in these woods today. She was not given to fighting with fists. She had other weapons, as she had always maintained. So too would she use them here, if she had to.

That was a choice she could make, and happily.

"You mistake me." Thorbrand gripped her harder, though she thrilled to the touch. "I thought a Mercian princess nothing more than a task to complete. A vow made to my king, so there was a kind of honor in the task, though it came with no glory. But this I vowed to do for him, as I would do whatever he asked."

"You are loyal," Aelfwynn said softly. "Most kings dream of your like, yet find instead men like those who abandoned me on that road."

He shook his head, his face grave. "I expected a shrew. A spoiled creature, no good for anything. I thought I would take this mewling chit to the cottage I had found and see how we would suit, only her and me. It would make no difference in the outcome, you understand. But before I set sail for the west, I needed to know if Aethelflaed's daughter could tend a fire. Bake a simple loaf of bread. Produce ale to drink."

"And what if I had failed you?" She was not certain she wanted his answer.

"If you could not do these simple tasks, I would still take you across the seas. But where we settled would be different. If you were useless, better I should take you to a village where our survival need not depend on what you could or could not do. But if you possessed even the most rudimentary skills, I would take you instead to the land I claimed as mine last summer."

She sniffed. "I hope I passed this…bride test."

"Aelfwynn." Thorbrand made a sound that could have been a laugh, though his gaze was far too serious. "You do not heed me. It took me less than one day to forget entirely that there was any test at all."

She allowed herself a small sigh, and liked well how the heat of his hands made her feel warm when she knew she was not. "That is no small thing, I suppose."

"There is more," he said in that same grave manner. "Living with you in that way, so far from the din of battle and the commands of kings... It reminded me that for all I dream of the glory that can be won with the swing of my sword, so too do I have other dreams." He reached up and ran his hand over the wild hair she wore braided now, as if she was one of them. A Northman's woman. *This* Northman's woman. "A quiet life. The love of a good woman. Land that is ours to work as we will, and whatever sons you may give me."

"Thorbrand..." she whispered.

"I have known nothing but shame for the want of such things," he told her solemnly. "For I have fought in too many battles. They have marked me well. The Irish warrior who left me with scars all over my side took more from me that day." He looked intense then. Tortured. She found her own fingers twitching as she thought of tracing over those scars like claws that raked down his side. His dark eyes blazed. "He killed my mother while I watched. I did nothing."

Aelfwynn made a low sound of sorrow, but he kept on.

"And as I lay there, bloody and useless, he took down my father, too." Thorbrand's face looked harder, then. His gaze bleaker. "I saw the look in his eyes as he died and knew well his disappointment in me."

"I do not believe it." Thorbrand's eyes widened, no doubt at her temerity. But Aelfwynn shook her head then, as decisively as if she was a queen in truth though her voice was soft. "I do not. His wife was dead. His son injured, and badly. Maybe his true disappointment was in himself."

For a long while, Thorbrand stared at her as if she really had sunk her dagger in deep. He looked nothing short of thunderstruck.

When he pulled in a breath, it sounded ragged to her ears. "I have carried this failure with me, Aelfwynn, always."

She slid her hands higher on his chest, and dared to place her palm over his heart. "Maybe it was never yours, Thorbrand."

He looked as if he were in pain. As if her

hands on him were setting him alight. "I have given myself to these wars on behalf of our people, over and over, that I might right those wrongs in some way. It has shamed me deeply that I might want anything but the battles and the glory that might bring honor to my family as I could not do, then." She shook her head again, but when she opened her mouth to speak, he stopped her. He gripped her that much tighter. He lowered that midnight gaze of his even closer. "Yet whether what you have suggested here is truth or a wish, I know well that I would walk away from all of it. I would do this happily for as long as we must stay away, and call it the better choice, because of you."

And Aelfwynn had spent long and lonely years learning how not to speak. How not to reveal herself. How to hide.

But this was Thorbrand, who thought himself a failure when the scars she'd seen on him suggested he had nearly died himself. He had offered her choices in that road. Not good choices, as he had said, but choices all the same. He had treated her tenderly when he did not have to. He planned to marry her. He had held her after she'd cut him with her dagger, and he had let her flail and fight until she could do no more, never crushing her or hurting her.

Just as he had taken her maidenhead in that pool, making her feel as if she had been the one to gift it to him. Not ruining her in the way she'd understood ruin, all sobs and repentance and horror, but leaving her wanting more.

And unless she was mistaken, he had, just now, given her a piece of himself he had never given another. He had made himself vulnerable in the telling. Aelfwynn knew, with a deep rush of feminine understanding, that if she did not comprehend and accept the gift he offered her here, she might never see it again.

That was more than she could bear.

Aelfwynn melted against him, and ordered herself, once and for all, to show that she was as brave and courageous as her mother had been. As she too had been, in her own way. But this mattered more to her than kingdoms in play or the whims of her uncle. Or Ragnall.

This meant everything.

This was Thorbrand's heart, and she intended to cherish it. And him.

She slid her arms up and around his neck,

stretching up on her toes and forgetting how they ached, and she held his gaze as if her very life depended on it.

For she knew well that it did.

More important, so too did her heart and any possibility of happiness.

"I told you once that I dreamed of peace," she told him softly. "Far away from disputed borders and fortified *burhs*. Out of reach of kings and would-be queens. Where the only blood that signifies is that we will share when we make our daughters."

He smiled at that. "Will we have daughters then? I can tell you, sweeting, if the daughters we raise are like their mother, I will know I have the favor of the gods after all."

She found that she was smiling too. "I never wished to be a queen, Thorbrand, or even a great lady as my mother was. I can think of nothing I should love more than to be your wife. To bear you sons and daughters in turn. And…" She paused, searching his face, but how could she keep back pieces of herself when he had shared his with her? What kind of marriage would that be? Maybe others resigned themselves to what was practical. But Aelfwynn was not *others,* and she wanted more. She wanted everything. "And I will love you, as best I can, for as long as we are given."

And everything stilled. Her heart and breath. Him. The wood around them, even the sun above.

"I will hold you to that, Aelfwynn," Thorbrand told her. His voice was rough, though his touch was gentle. And the look in his eyes made tears form in hers. "And when Ragnall calls for us, I will remind him that we are kin. And I will ask of him—"

"No," Aelfwynn said fiercely. "That is not who you are. When your king calls, we will do as he bids. That is the vow you made and so it is our honor that is at stake. *Our* honor. And I will not have you stain it, Thorbrand. Not for anything."

"You are fierce, little Saxon, are you not?" But his voice was filled with something like wonder.

"I was raised to believe that weaving peace is a woman's sacred duty, not only to her family, new and old, but to God." Aelfwynn thought of the women who had taught her, Mildrithe and Aethelflaed in their turn. Two such different women. Two markedly different places in the world, and each had known precisely where she belonged. Aelfwynn had always envied them that knowledge, but she felt it now. Here, in Thorbrand's arms, at last. "How could I consider myself a good woman, much less a good wife, if I did not make certain to keep, woven tight and gleaming, my husband's duty to his king?"

"I do not deserve you," he gritted out, and she heard a kind of pain in those words. She wanted to reel at that. At the notion this huge, hard man who she had once thought terrifying might truly believe the words he spoke.

Then again, he truly believed he had failed his own parents.

"But you do," she replied swiftly, her voice still fierce and her gaze steady on his. "For so you claimed me in the middle of an old road and made me yours. Does a man deserve what he claims? Our kings would say they do, I think. And so must I."

"Sweeting," Thorbrand said, his voice almost too rough then. Too deep. Yet it moved in her as if it was a part of her. As if he was. "Aelfwynn. I will make you a good husband, I promise you. Whether we till the land or sit high above your homeland, it will be the same. I promise you this. And more, I will love you.

With my body, my sword, and my heart, and every blessing the gods have ever granted me. So do I swear here and now."

Aelfwynn reached over and pulled his dagger out, smiling when she saw his dark brows rise. But instead of swinging it in his direction, she shook back the sleeve of her cloak, and pricked herself on the inside of her wrist. Deep enough only to let a small droplet of blood rise against her pale skin.

Then, holding his gaze, she fitted her wound to his.

"Blood spells are a dangerous game," Thorbrand warned her, though his gaze was warm. "What would your priests say?"

"I don't care," she replied. She held their forearms together, then she gazed up at him. "I don't want to wait for our daughters and sons to come, Thorbrand. The only blood that matters is ours. Here, now, we have made ourselves one."

"Aelfwynn," he ground out. "I love you."

"As I love you, Thorbrand," she whispered back.

This time, he took her with him down to the ground. He laid upon his cloak, but settled her above and astride him. So that her cloak could keep them warm as, there on the forest floor with winter all around, he made her his wife.

He showed her his love, as she showed him hers, their gazes locked together as if they had been blind until this moment.

No hiding. No fighting.

No wars or kings or games. Just the two of them made one, at last.

They whispered words of forever as Aelfwynn took Thorbrand inside her once again. And then slowly, their fingers linked and their eyes full of only and ever each other, she married him in every way that mattered, there on the forest floor.

With only winter as witness.

And a love so bright it felt to them like spring.

Chapter Fifteen

⦿⟡⦿

*Ful oft wit beotedan þæt unc ne gedælde
nemne deað ana, owiht elles.*

Very often we two vowed that we would
not be parted except by death alone, nothing else.

—from *The Wife's Lament*,
translated by Eleanor Parker

But the magic they'd made together in the
woods was only the first wedding that day.

"Weddings require preparation," Aelfwynn
argued. They had dressed anew, and Thorbrand
had yet lingered. He'd settled Aelfwynn before
him and tended to her hair, combing it out with
his fingers and then braiding it back so that
no trace of wildness or the woods remained.
"Negotiations between families take time."

"Sweeting." He turned her to look at him again, his midnight gaze bright with laughter. "Our negotiations are well and truly concluded."

"It is winter. No one marries in winter—for how can the families make such a long trip when the weather—?"

"Aelfwynn. If your family came to this wedding it would be a war."

She blinked at that, then took a deep, shaky breath. "Indeed. Indeed, it would."

And she knew his face so well it might as well have been carved into her heart. Yet still did she sigh a little at what she saw on it then, a tenderness she knew well was only hers.

Only and ever hers.

He smoothed a hand over the hair he had fixed to his liking, then smiled.

And her worries eased.

Because the wedding they would have today was for the world. For the benefit of kings. Their truth was here. In these cold woods so like the forest where they had met. Where wolves might howl and snow threaten, but Thorbrand would keep them safe. And she would weave love and laughter all around them, and make them whole.

Over and over again, no matter what they were called to do.

They made it back to the village while the sun was still high. Thorbrand marched Bjørn before him, so that all might know his misdeeds and witness his punishment as he led him back to face Ragnall's harsh justice.

But such justice was to remain the province of Ragnall and his men, for Aelfwynn was immediately taken in hand by the village women she had befriended the day before. They chattered to her of the mead they had prepared, the honey brought from Ragnall's own stores, just as he had provided the beasts for feasting and sacrifice. And Aelfwynn wanted to find the customs they spoke of so easily horrifying unto her soul, but in truth, she did not. For had she not moved without thought in the woods earlier? Had she not performed what Thorbrand had called *blood magic?*

She had listened to dour priests the whole of her life and none of her prayers had warded off the Northman she would marry this day. None of her piety had saved her, and her sacrifice—the sin her priests would have called a stain upon her soul—had brought her a greater joy than any she had ever known. More than simply joy, it had given her the purpose she had always desired. Thorbrand had seemed to her a demon sent to plague her at first, yet had become more dear to her than her own heart, and in so doing had answered all of her prayers. Each and every one, and then some. How could she think it anything but God's will?

Her spiritual concerns assuaged thus, she permitted the village women to treat her like one of them. They drew her a bath and spoke to her of what went on between a man and a woman, not simply in bed, but in life. The older woman from the day before met her gaze frankly, answering questions without waiting for Aelfwynn to ask them. The other women rinsed her with herb-scented water, then helped her dress in a new gown that announced to all that she was not the same woman who had come to this village. For she was to leave it again as Thorbrand's wife.

"*Inn mátki munr,*" the women murmured approvingly. The great passion.

Love, Aelfwynn thought as they led her outside again, where Ragnall himself waited to play the part of her family in the wedding ritual. Love had made them one. Love would protect and keep them. Love, not war.

Whatever came next, she and Thorbrand would do it together.

"Are you ready, sweeting?" Thorbrand asked quietly when she reached his side, the whole world in his gaze.

She smiled at him, bold and bright and recklessly smitten, and cared not who saw it or what they might think of her. All that mattered was that he love her, and he did. "I cannot wait."

After the feasting and the wedding night, they returned to their little, remote cottage with the ceremonial gifts they had given each other, swords for their sons and the coronet Aelfwynn had worn at the wedding for their daughters, and a month's supply of the mead that they must drink with attendant formality until it were gone.

"I did not think to see this place again," Aelfwynn said softly in the sweet heat of the spring-fed pool, wrapped up in Thorbrand's arms. "I had resigned myself to its loss."

Thorbrand smiled down at her, his face open and intent in that manner that still set Aelfwynn's heart to beating, hard and fast, for it was only for her. He had taken his time with her hair here, combing it out with his fingers as he liked to do, taking it down from the braids wrapped around her head that showed she was a married woman at a glance. Her long hair, now, was for his eyes alone.

She found she liked well all these ways that she belonged to him.

Thorbrand held her aloft in the warm water and tucked a heavy coil of her wet hair behind her ear. "They say, do they not, that it is a good thing indeed to love what good things you can."

"If it is your heart's desire," Aelfwynn replied, for she too knew this wisdom.

"You are more than my heart's desire, sweeting," he said, his voice rough with the emotion she knew well he showed only her. And so would she cherish it, and him. "You are my very heart."

"And you mine, Thorbrand."

He took her there, the way he had taken her first. Her cries echoed back to her from the hills. His arms held her as he moved within her, slick and deep.

Until they made themselves one, just as they most desired it.

They waited for spring in the cottage, safely out of reach of the designs of kings and armies. And when winter released its grip on the land and the earth began to thaw, they left the cottage that would always be their first home, to Aelfwynn's mind, one last time. This time they rode into York, where Ragnall now ruled undisputed and a ship waited to take them to the land far west.

Aelfwynn knew she was already thickening as she climbed onboard the vessel built to carry settlers and cargo alike that day, a secret she suspected her husband already knew, so well did he know her curves. She felt sure their baby would come after summer passed, when the weather turned cold once more, and they would become a family, far away on foreign shores.

A better family than the one she left behind, she could not help but think.

For I will fight for you, she promised the small life inside her. *Not for land or glory. And I am the daughter of kings and queens. I promise you, I will win.*

They set out on a pretty spring day, leaving behind the clatter of York to make their way along the River Ouse and to the cold North

Sea. She and Thorbrand would welcome their first child—a son, she knew, though she could not have said how she knew it—in a place she'd not yet seen. They would live a life she did not yet know, certain to be different than the many versions of a life she left here.

Yet she had Thorbrand, and that was all that mattered. For because of him, the idea of an uncertain future did not unsettle her. Not anymore. She knew well that whatever happened, and whatever came, they would face it together. The caprice of kings, the ravages of weather and time, all of this was as nothing as long as they had each other.

So it was that Aelfwynn, only daughter of Aethelflaed, Lady of the Mercians, settled in for her voyage away from the ancestral lands of her people with salt on her face and the wind at their back.

And did not look behind her.

Chapter Sixteen

❧

Gammel kjærleik rustar ikkje.

Old love does not corrode.

—Old Norse Proverb

Iceland, 922

Three years later, a stranger came to the small, coastal settlement on the great island called Ísland where Thorbrand and Aelfwynn had made their home. And better yet, had started their own farm.

"You are the man I seek," the stranger said when Thorbrand, having seen him coming from a distance, invited the man inside the longhouse he had built with the help of his far-flung neighbors in the hope that one day, more of his kin would find their way here. "I come with news of Ragnall."

Aelfwynn tended to the central hearth, their hall warm against the remnants of fog without, and Thorbrand could tell by the demure way she kept her gaze averted that she was as stricken by the stranger's words as he was.

For they had always known this day would come.

They had prepared for this, Thorbrand thought. And yet, somehow, he felt as wholly unprepared as if he was green and young and had faced an Irish warrior he'd never had a hope of besting. When he was none of those things, not any longer.

Ever mindful of his place in this dark, brutal world and the promises he had made, Thorbrand had not allowed his training to desert him here. He had made a vow to his king and so would he keep it, and that meant he must be ready to fight when called. Thorbrand knew how to keep his sword blade sharp and his fighting instincts honed. He knew how to keep himself a warrior.

Even if, as season followed season and winter sat heavier still than it had in the other places he'd lived, he considered himself less and less a warrior. And more and more a man who planted and plowed and honored the land he'd claimed.

He and Aelfwynn had made a very different life than any he could have imagined when he had been a small boy with his father's storied deeds in his ears and a heart for what battle might bring him, gold and glory alike. They had spent their first summer building on the land he'd claimed and preparing for the winter that was never too far off on this cold island. She had given him a son that first fall, another a year later, and was yet thick again. There could be no doubt that the gods had blessed them, and well.

And here, where there were black sand beaches and gods in the mountainsides, the two of them worked together, woven into one. She worked a kind of magic, his Saxon princess, who sounded less and less Mercian with every year. Aelfwynn laughed when she told him how her stitches had failed her as a girl in a royal court, when her hardy sewing, capable weaving, and all the mending she did suited their life here perfectly. Simple and stalwart, as so too was she.

Each of his sons had been born into his hands. Each had chosen to fight his way into the world in the middle of a snowstorm. Thorbrand had no doubt that the next would be the same, a bright red howl on a cold night, Aelfwynn made of gold and valor as she labored and then nursed these children they had made.

He could not understand why there were no songs of these battles women fought, each dangerous and beautiful. Thorbrand had already loved her. But with each day, each season, each birth, he only loved her the more.

And he had expected the work. He had longed for the quiet. He had expected his beautiful nights with his wife, and hungered for any other time he could get his hands on her, for his need of her only grew. Many a night they would sit near the fire and he would play with her hair while she rocked their babes to sleep. Or better yet, once she succeeded, he would play the games he liked best. After their time in the cottage in Northumbria, he had known well that their life together was a pleasure, and the hard work they did only made the pleasure greater.

What he had not expected was the laughter. He had not expected to watch her nurse his son at her breast, then meet her gaze and know in that moment that the whole of the world, all its blood and its battles, its conquerors and kings, were nothing compared to this.

To the love that ran in him, more powerful than all the seas he had crossed.

And now this stranger stood before him, bearing the standard of the man he called his king. Thorbrand had no interest at all in returning to the life he'd left behind him. Everything in him rebelled. He had given no thought to territorial disputes across the sea while he had beaten out a life here. He had trained, but he had allowed himself to think of his own land, for a change.

Not the land he could only and ever hold at Ragnall's pleasure.

But he had made his vows long ago. And he was a man of honor or he was no man.

There was only one possible response.

For surely it mattered not what a man felt in his heart, only what actions he took. How he honored his promises. How he served his king.

"Then you are come to me a friend," Thorbrand said to the stranger. "I await Ragnall's commands with gladness."

Aelfwynn lifted her head from her work then, her hands stilling over her stitching. Yet he could see the flash of her gold gaze from across the room. His prize far greater than coins. His hoard far better than any dragon's.

She did not need to speak. She would not. Yet he knew her heart as well as he did his own.

It was as she had promised him long ago. They were who they were. She was the daughter of Aethelflaed, heir to Mercia whether her uncle liked it or did not. He was sworn to his king's side, come what might.

They had always agreed, since that day in the cold wood where they'd bound themselves in blood, that when the time came they would do what they must. He might not have failed his parents as he'd imagined all these years, and he would not do so now. Honor was all, or they were nothing, and how could he raise his sons to be good, strong men if he shirked his?

Yet he could admit to himself that he had wished for more time.

He braced himself.

"Is my sad duty to inform you that Ragnall, King of Jorvik, has died," the stranger told him, his voice formal. "His cousin Sitric has taken his place and though Edward of Wessex advances, there is no need for you to make good on the vows you made."

Thorbrand signaled Aelfwynn for ale, and sat with his visitor. And was moved, as ever, to watch the graceful way his wife moved. To watch as she filled their cups, all that was feminine and lovely, making it clear without a word that this was a fine home and Thorbrand a powerful leader in his own right, or how could he boast such a woman as Aelfwynn?

He had grown more and more attuned to the work women did, here in this remote place where no act was ever unseen. And vowed that someday, he would make certain that he and his sons, at the least, sang Aelfwynn the songs she deserved.

Songs that might die with them, belonging only to their family, for there were some secrets that must never be told—and what had happened to Aethelflaed's daughter must always be one of them.

Thorbrand sat with his visitor for some time, as the messenger told him the story of Ragnall, his death, and the rest of the news from lands across the sea that Thorbrand did not intend to see again. Not in this life.

Much later, when the stranger had gone out to relieve himself, Thorbrand sat, his gaze on his cup, when he felt his wife's touch.

"You loved him well," she said softly at his ear, her arms around his shoulders. "This is a blow."

And Thorbrand knew he would grieve this loss in the days and years to come. Ragnall had been more to him than a king or even a surrogate father. He had guided him, molded him. Thorbrand would tell his sons many stories about the battles Ragnall had fought. He would teach them what a king was, using Ragnall as his example, for Ragnall had made Thorbrand the man he was.

A man who recognized what he had, and deeply appreciated what was lost, but did not mourn the dead at the cost of the living.

Because there was only so much life a man had, and it mattered not how he fought or what he wished, for only fate knew when it ended.

Thorbrand had no intention of wasting a moment of this life he'd built. Not one single moment, and especially not now his life was finally his.

He tumbled Aelfwynn into his lap and laughed at the little sound she made. Then he smiled at her, drinking in her eyes of the finest gold even as his hands moved to mold themselves over her fuller breasts and the mound of her belly where his son yet grew.

"Sweeting," he said, as if it were a prayer. "My love. Did you not hear? We are free."

"Silly man," she said quietly, melting into him the way she always did. The way she always would. "Since the moment you first saw me, then took me, then neglected to mention I was not your slave."

"It is easily reversed, this marriage," he teased her, as he often did. "If a slave is what you would prefer to be for me."

"Thorbrand," Aelfwynn said, putting her hand over his mouth and laughing when he kissed it. "We have ever been free. Together we can never be anything else."

And so it was, from that day forward.

Woven through with that bright love, boundless laughter, and the flame that burned hotter in both of them, one season after the next, until it felt like fate, after all.

* * * * *

MILLS & BOON

Coming next month

A PROPOSAL TO RISK THEIR FRIENDSHIP
Louise Allen

He could let go and Melissa would lift her head and those warm, soft lips would no longer be clinging to his ... and this kiss would end. And he did not want that.

Nor, it seemed, did Melissa. It was an inexperienced kiss, he could tell. Her mouth remained closed, but she made a little purring sound deep in her throat and every primitive male instinct demanded that he turn that purr into a moan.

Henry sat up. Where he got the willpower from he had no idea, but there they were suddenly, somewhat breathless and, in his case, most inconveniently aroused.

'That was very quick thinking,' he said when his brain allowed speech.

'I hope it was convincing,' Melissa said. 'I have absolutely no practical experience of that kind of thing.'

'Of course not. I think you may be certain that they suspected nothing,' he said.

'It was the only thing I could think of to stop them seeing your face,' she went on, looking round. She located her hat and blew dust from it. 'I think there is no permanent damage, thank goodness.'

Not to the hat, at any rate. What was the matter with him? He had been kissed by lovers of great experience. One innocent pressing her lips to his as part of a charade could hardly weigh against those encounters. Melissa was a friend, not a lover. An innocent, not a woman of the world.

A friend. We have something special—do not ruin this.

'Have they gone, do you think?' Melissa asked.

Henry looked out. 'They are walking away. No point in trying to catch them up.'

'No, I suppose not.' She put her hat back on and tied the ribbons in a rather lopsided bow.

Without thinking, Henry went across and retied it. How had he not noticed her scent before? 'Rosemary?' He realised he had said it out loud.

Melisa looked perplexed, then laughed. 'Oh, my hair rinse. That tickles.'

'What? Oh, sorry.' His fingers were still on the bow, touching the smooth skin under her chin. He removed his hand as casually as he could. 'It is safe to follow now, I think.'

A lot safer than staying here. Melissa is a friend, he reminded himself as he followed her out of the summer-house. *She trusts you, as a friend, not to be reacting like this to her, not to be thinking about her scent, the feel of her. Her mouth.*

Continue reading
A PROPOSAL TO RISK THEIR FRIENDSHIP
Louise Allen

Available next month
www.millsandboon.co.uk

COMING SOON!

We really hope you enjoyed reading this book.
If you're looking for more romance, be sure to
head to the shops when new books are
available on

Thursday 27th May